SLOW EMERGENCIES

SLOW EMERGENCIES

Nancy Huston

STEERFORTH PRESS
SOUTH ROYALTON, VERMONT

For information about permission to reproduce
selections from this book, write to:
Steerforth Press, L.C.
PO Box 70, South Royalton, Vermont 05068

LIBRARY OF CONGRESS CATALOGING-IN-PUBLICATION DATA

Huston, Nancy, 1953–
  [Virevolte. English]
  Slow emergencies / Nancy Huston.
      p.   cm.
  ISBN 1-883642-63-9 (alk. paper)
      I. Title.

PQ3919.2.H87 V5813 2001
843'.914—dc21   00-046370

FIRST AMERICAN EDITION

For Denis Hirson,
third person present

and with thanks to
Catherine Atlani,
Marie and Roberte Léger

*"What is dance, if not
the stifled essence of a scream?"*

R. M. RILKE

Part One

THE SOLOIST

That body is out of her.

A girl, say the people whose hands are now skillfully manip-
ulating tiny angular limbs and lumps of glistening sticky but-
tocks and hairy head down there, then plunging deep into the
yawning chasm of Lin's body to extract the black-red pulsating form of living flesh that belongs to no one, neither to her
nor to the child — then they are sewing her.

Lin does not care what they do to her now. That body is
out of her. It is on the roof of its empty house and its lips have
fastened round her nipple and are sucking fast as heartbeat,
fierce as sex. A person behaving like a real live baby and
daughtering her. Such a wee wisp of a thing whereas it had
weighed like a boulder in her gut. While the wolf was sleeping, bloated and ill from having gobbled down seven baby
goats one after the other without so much as bothering to
chew them, the nanny goat came to the rescue of her children: she slit open the wolf's stomach with a knife and all
seven kids jumped out safe and sound, then they filled his
stomach with stones and stitched it back up again and when
the wolf awoke, oh my *God* . . . But here the stone has been

replaced by a kid instead of the other way around, and the torn flesh is being sewed up and Lin is a mother. Not only that, but Derek is a father. His nervous futile fanning of her face and smoothing of her hair has ceased; now one of his hands is squeezing hers and he has laid the other gently on his daughter's minute white-clad back. So many monumental new terms coming into play here. A few seconds ago there was no such thing as daughter mother father and now there they are, these words have been violently promoted from clichés to Beethoven symphonies, choirs of angels, floods of sunlight. The nurse is still stitching and dabbing down there, the sting and pierce of the needle are pleasant to Lin, compared with the just-past hellish upheaval of self.

Once rinsed of womb muck and pressed dry with a towel, Angela's fine thin hair is blond. Her head nests in the crook of Lin's left arm as her lips pump imperiously to draw from Lin's breast the thin nourishing liquid which is not yet milk. Her eyes stare into Lin's eyes as though each second of staring brought with it as much newness and replenishment as each second of sucking.

Voraciously Angela gulps down the look in her mother's eyes.

The ward is a swarm of cries and coos and cuddles. Other mothers press small squalling mouths to dripping nipples. Get out of my happiness, thinks Lin.

Angela is the only baby on earth and Lin the only mother.

How could she not know to swab the stub of scabbed flesh at her own daughter's midriff?

In the shower, Lin soaps and scrubs her empty body, vigorously beneath the armpits, gingerly between the legs. She is still there. She did not die or become someone else. Not only is she still herself but she is also a mother. Not only is she still alive but someone else is also, totally, alive at the far end of the corridor and she can feel the tug of that person's life at her heartstrings. It is like falling in love only without the darkness, without the thrill and clutch of fear.

Angela's feet. Those same feet which a thousand times had kicked Lin soft-thud strangely in the stomach, bladder, intestines, lungs. Long curved toes, nearly invisible slits of toenails, wrinkles everywhere. Absurdly large coming at the end of such puny calves and thighs, absurdly small next to any pair of shoes. Except the pastel booties knit by Derek's mother, Violet, with ribbons slipped through the ankle stitches to tie them securely but despite the ribbons the great red feet keep pushing them off, the left one is always waving around naked and chill, undressed by the snug smug right.

Bathing her. Lin's left arm crooked beneath Angela's upper back, supporting her head, her right hand gently sponging the fat stomach, sponging the frog legs parted in fifth-position grand plié, sponging the unspeakably sweet sex. Angela's big eyes follow every twitch and twinkle of the face above her. And she is so at home in the tepid water, so ecstatically abandoned.

During her daughter's long spans of white sleep Lin often finds the clinic's exercise room empty and can lie splayed on its hardwood floor, contract-release relaxing, getting reaccustomed to being the only person in her body. Sometimes when she sits and bends, forward forward downward, drops of milk seep through her shirt and spatter her naked knees.

You'll be back on stage in no time, Mrs. Lhomond, the nurse says one day, upon seeing her emerge from the exercise room. Lin nods, radiant.

They slip the fabulous bulk of the *Sunday Times* into the stroller bag, where it almost upends their little girl. They laugh. They are inclined to laugh at the slightest pretext.

Angela is asleep, swaddled in woolen blankets, her eyes protected from the sun. On the park bench, as their hands are occupied and dirtied with the newspaper, they hold feet, legs twined.

Look at those families, says Lin after a while. I mean, just look at them.

The other babies are hopelessly pudgy, they are dressed in garish synthetic pinks and yellows and blues, to say nothing of the new green recently concocted by the clothing industry, the only green it had never in a million years entered nature's head to produce. Angela's clothes and blankets by contrast are shimmering mist, water lilies, cloud formations. All the babies over the age of one — all the walking babies — are monstrous: they look like circus giants or men on stilts, like adults pretending to be babies. Their mothers chitchat on benches, yell orders at their offspring and filch their cookies when their backs are turned.

Lin points.

You see? The woman's absorbed in feeding mashed bananas to her son and the man is watching teenaged girls swish by and looking sheepish. He's got to sit there feigning an interest in his chubby grubby offspring secretly he's thinking Jesus, if only I could slip through these bench slats here while Mathilda isn't looking . . .

The worst of it, says Derek, is that if he hadn't been such a funky dancer in the first place, pushing and pressing and breathing down Martha's neck and insisting on going all the way, there would have been no gurgling BillyBob Junior sitting in that there perambulator.

They kiss.

That would have been one empty pram, man, says Lin. A pity to leave it empty, says Derek, what with those aesthetically alternating white-and-yellow stripes and all.

They kiss.

But don't those wispy slips of girls make you wanna get up and go, too?

Oh . . . I waited a long time for perfection to come along, you know, says Derek.

If you can call that sort of behavior waiting, says Lin.

They kiss and kiss, their tongues in each other's mouths. Angela wakes and they rock her stroller gently, kissing and kissing.

The shit is fine. They compete to see which of them can wipe Angela's ass the cleanest the fastest. They kiss her white rump, rubbing their cheeks against her smooth-as-glass soft-as-silk skin. Angela's face is calm and serious when they change her.

Lin loves to watch her husband's hands, the hands of a philosophy professor, undo the snap buttons of her pajamas, pop pop pop all six of them, withdraw her great red feet and remove her soiled diaper, carefully part and clean the tiny folds of her vulva, wiping downward from sex to anus and never the reverse, powder her dry and rediaper her and slip her feet back into the pajama feet and do up the snap buttons again, all six of them click click click.

Her own inner flesh is raw and tender, her breasts swollen and blue-veined, she cannot yet take him inside the cave from which the baby burst but he is in no hurry, the sight of that volcano, that churning bleeding living knot of flesh, had awed him as the burning bush awed Moses so they float in sensual limbo, find pleasure with their mouths, fingers, skin, weep sometimes for no reason whatsoever.

With friends, they refer to Angela as they have always heard parents refer to their children: casually. Sometimes they even force themselves to complain about her feedings in the middle of the night. This nonchalance, they think, must be part of an enormous parently plot to keep nonparents in the dark.

Theresa arrives after breakfast three times a week, with her apron and house slippers in a plastic bag, to clean the dirt Lin and her family leave behind. She is Italian, in her forties. Some families, Theresa had told Lin, expect her to handwash soiled underwear, scrape pots and pans coated with burned-stiff week-old food, comb dog hairs out of cushions. Here it is fairly clean cleaning she has to do.

Lin is in her dance room, the spacious attic with its slants
and rafters and skylights and wall of mirrors and hardwood
floor, which was the first room she and Derek had renovated
when they bought the house. She pulls on her thick old
woolen socks with the heels and toes cut out of them. This is
the first time.

Excited, she moves to the barre. Slowly opens and oils
her joints. Yes she can again bend over from the waist with
her legs straight and place her elbows on the floor. Yes she
can again put her foot on the wall high above her head and
press her face to her knee. Little by little her arms and legs
lengthen and her back dilates — she is a giant.

Usually after an hour of work she enters the place where
it is no longer she who produces the dance but the dance that
produces her, the dance that takes hold of her feet and arms
and waist and spins and holds her, retains and releases her as
it pleases.

Oh this silent thing, this contradiction in terms
this transfiguration of body into soul
this art of the perishable flesh
this ephemeral eternity
But today the warmup is enough to drain her completely.
At eleven o'clock she curls up in a corner of the dance room
and draws a bath towel over her body.

They have found day care for Angela. Late each afternoon, either Lin or Derek is allowed to enter a roomful of little people and extract one of them as theirs and take it home.

Lin enters Angela's room and kneels on the floor next to her crib. She listens to the evenness of her daughter's breathing. All this is so good. Lin is never afraid that Angela will die in her sleep. She never hovers over her crib to make sure she has not stopped breathing.

Derek! cries Lin — so loudly that Angela wakens with a start. Derek! She turned over in her crib! She turned over by herself, I swear it! I put her down on her back and now she's on her stomach — come and see, come and see!

Lin and Derek join hands and prance around their daughter's bedroom. Her wobbly head raised, Angela watches them wide-eyed, uncertain whether the hubbub is a good or a bad sign.

They put her on her back again. She struggles, teeters, plops to her stomach.

They applaud wildly and put her on her back again.

But Angela is exhausted — try as she might, kicking and straining, red-faced with fury, she cannot turn over a third time.

Rachel drops by with a gift of black pajamas for Angela, and Lin knows what this means; it is a reminder of the ancient love of death between the two of them, the penchant that had soldered them together for so many years. A shiver goes through her the first time she fastens the darkness round her daughter's nape of curls, but the result is irrefutable.

In high school they had recognized each other instantly: excellent grades, dark rings under the eyes, a keen taste for silence. Like a pair of sinister twins they had dressed in tight black clothes, been wan and drawn and pale and tense together, smoked fifty cigarettes a day and starved themselves to skeletal skinniness because they wished to hover at the very edge of existence, as close to the bone as possible. They had not asked to live and their interest in life was feigned and forced. If they absolutely had to live, they preferred to do so as quickly as possible and get it over with, so they worked themselves to the point of collapse in a state of frenzied indifference, Lin at her dance and Rachel at her Greek philosophers, desiring perfection only because it was tantamount to death. They ate skimpily and irregularly, smoked not despite but because of the fact they knew it was bad for them, especially Lin, preferring the poison of danger to the vapid complacency of good health, filling time to its utmost limit, getting up each day at dawn, eschewing naps and holidays, sensing nonetheless the scraping tick of seconds at their backs and resenting each of them individually.

It was not that their ideals had been tarnished — no, they had never had ideals because they had never had mothers.

Lin's had been whisked off to heaven by a brain hemorrhage
when she was barely three, and Rachel's had turned from her
in disgust the minute she had glimpsed her baby's sex — a
daughter could never replace the scholarly European uncles
and cousins and grandfathers who had been gassed at
Birkenau. Both girls had gone on living out of sheer inertia.
They could not instinctively take care of their bodies because
their bodies had always been handled by loveless females.
They had learned slowly, as from a user's manual, the objec-
tive rules of what was good and bad for them, and usually did
the latter. God did not exist, their fathers did not care, and
there were as yet no husbands on the horizon; since no one
exercised authority over them, they gradually themselves
became authority incarnate, slave driver and slave strapped
together in the same body, the same mind.

Rachel had remained true to their shared philosophy
— succeed in everything, believe in nothing. Lin had
betrayed it.

She now believes in playing peek-a-boo with Angela.
She does it wholeheartedly, whereas the agreement between
her and Rachel was that they had no hearts.

Fifty times in a row, Angela covers her head with a towel
and calls herself — Aaaaa-laaaa! Fifty times in a row, Lin
gently pulls the towel away. Fifty times in a row, Angela
bursts into delighted laughter. And so does Lin, though they
are not laughing for the same reasons.

In Rachel's eyes, she can see awareness of her betrayal but
no reproach.

Drink this and your fishtail will turn into a pair of human legs. Eat this and you will suddenly grow very tall. Put this in your pocket and you will become invisible. Make love with this man and before you know it there will be a baby, live and kicking in its crib in front of you. It is incredible, impossible, thinks Lin.

It's all an illusion, Isadora had written to the father of her first child, Deirdre. *But the baby isn't an illusion. She's lovely.*

Lin pours the coffee. Very black for Rachel and half milk for herself.

You don't smoke anymore? Rachel asks.

Come on, I hate conversations about smoking and not smoking, they're as bad as conversations about computers. Just smoke, I don't care.

Now that you mention it, I had a dream about my computer the other night.

Go to hell.

No, seriously — I was sitting there working at my computer and all of a sudden the text just vanished and this enormous mouth appeared on the screen with the printed message: I'M HUNGRY! Only if I fed it a nice fat dictionary would it go on processing words for me; otherwise it would conk out on me for good. Well, since I didn't have a dictionary handy, I grabbed a bunch of old phone books and stuffed them down its throat.

The two woman laugh together, more loudly than usual.

You look so happy, Lin, says Rachel at length.

Yeah, I know. It worries me.

Well, it would have worried me if it hadn't worried you.

Oh, Rachel, I feel just great. It's terrifying.

Boy, I really sympathize.

Motherhood's not at all what it's touted out to be.

In other words?

Oh, you know . . . women in their kitchens, doing dirty deeds . . . regressing to infancy with their infants . . . Dowdy dames with their hair in curlers . . .

And their feet in slippers . . .

And their minds in soap . . .

Slipping into daydreams . . .

Losing hope . . .

Slapping their children's faces . . .

And making up their own . . .

Yeah, making themselves up — from scratch.

Again they laugh. Then Rachel says,

Hey, we can still be friends, you know, even if you're happy.

Angela is five months old and Lin has eaten her.

She had wanted to relive the pregnancy, having the baby inside of her, and especially the sheer roaring maelstrom when Angela had finally burst forth huge and wet.

The ingestion itself was not frightening — there was no blood, and roasting in the oven had diminished the baby's bulk, leaving scarcely a mouthful. Only afterward, when it is too late, does Lin realize that this method of impregnation will never work and that she has irrevocably destroyed her daughter. She screams, silently, until Angela's morning whimper jolts her awake and she leaps from bed.

Soon Angela will stop turning her face automatically when she feels her mother's breast against her cheek.

There is a new dance dying to be born within her and as always she is sick with fear as she approaches it and allows the images to proliferate. She will use Susie, the young black dancer, as the daughter. Susie will be sleeping in a corner of the stage wrapped in yards and yards of pure white tulle. A baby swaddled. Then she will rise, swaying, spinning slowly to unwrap the tulle. A baby swaddled. The she will rise, swaying, spinning slowly to unwrap the tulle, which turns out to be her wedding veil. Now she is no longer a baby but a woman, she is twisting, tied, trapped within the veil, a mummy swathed alive for marriage. As she struggles to free herself, her mouth will open in a silent endless scream. And Avital, who plays her mother, will rush to her assistance, press her daughter's body to her own and sway with her, enlacing her. The mother's long hair will get entangled in the swathes of cloth — all of this so slow, so slow — rivulets of tears will glide down her cheeks and mingle with the mesh of hair and tulle — but now the daughter is detaching herself, breaking away and dancing on her own — free and beautiful — leaving Avital alone as the veil wraps round her body more and more tightly — her shroud . . . She sinks to the floor and dies.

This is one scene, this could be lovely;

Somehow it must be ready in a month.

Angela, where are you?

It is the first time Lin has pronounced these words. Her daughter has gone squirming through the doorway like a caterpillar, arms and thighs and stomach propelling her out of Lin's sight.

One day Lin comes downstairs for lunch at one and Theresa is still there, only halfway through the ironing. Her cheeks are puffy and inflamed with weeping, her eyes dart like panicked animals trapped. Suddenly Lin shudders with longing for a life of pain and difficulty, noisy messy dinners with family members arguing hotly and laughing raucously and waving their hands in the air

The permanently blackened hands of her father, Joe, with their fingerprints and lifelines brought out by grease and motor oil, never waved in the air — not unless they were clenched into fists or unless he'd won at poker — yes, then they might triumphantly brandish bouquets of dollar bills beneath her nose at two in the morning, after the sprawling brawling card games during which she pretended to be asleep on her cot in the corner of the room. Through her eyelashes Lin would watch her stepmother, Bess, rip off her sweater in the heat of the bidding and scream with laughter as one of the men shoved his hand down her bra, ostensibly in search of an extra ace, while her father slammed his glass onto the table and announced Ladies and gentlemen, the name of the game is Flaming Cross! When she awoke of a Sunday morning, two or three players would often be passed out next to her on the floor, pants unbuckled, bristly jowls sagging, and to make her way to the bathroom she would have to skirt the reeking bodies on tiptoe.

They find it difficult to believe that someday, in addition to all her other miraculous abilities, Angela is also going to talk.

The rehearsals are going badly, partly because Susie, the young black dancer, is so very very good. She is small and sinewy, almost scrawny, almost a little girl you could walk past in a slum without a glance — sullen, extinguished, next to invisible — and then, the instant she starts moving, her body and face are lit up from within and the stage is suddenly abloom with beauty. Susie's natural grace makes the dancers around her look like amateurs, like people to whom it has just this minute occurred that they can do something nonfunctional with their bodies — her hands and feet are long, bony, prehensile, there must be at least seven joints to her fingers instead of three and she can pick up things with her feet as if they were hands — her wrists flick in, flick out and their position is always precisely right, always filled with meaning — a burst of poetry in the midst of prose.

Stop, says Lin. Take it again.

Okay, stop, says Lin. Take it again.

Again, says Lin.

Again.

Sixty, seventy times in the course of the afternoon, Lin

asks that Avital and Susie repeat a single spin — a movement that will eventually occupy three seconds of the dance, performed how many times in front of how many jaded spectators? — but it doesn't matter, she always tells her dancers. So much of our existence is haphazard, we put up with so much junk and waste, so much lip flapping and sloppiness — something somewhere must be exactly right, some tiny place preserved for the sacred, some homage paid to perfection — close, close as close as humanly possible, closer —
Form! Lin admonishes them. The form must be clear-cut and inevitable as the V of migrating birds

Avital is growing impatient, red in the face. She knows the repetitions are because of her. Lin can tell that her humiliation is turning into resentment; she must make sure it gets reconverted into energy for the dance, not spilled into words of anger or squelched into bitter silence.
Could you take it again, please?

No one can dance with Lin who has not learned to swallow pride and accept whole afternoons of pitiless criticism. Pride is for after the performance, not before.

This *care*. This unbelievable, incommensurable, insane attention to detail.

They are preparing dinner, Angela has four teeth, she is banging her plastic bowl on the tray of her high chair with a spoon and singing. Outside, snow falls and falls. Lin strains boiled carrots, transfers them from colander to bowl and mashes them with a fork; they are still bright orange, soft but not mushy; she adds a little butter and a little salt and a tiny pinch of sugar, then puts an egg on to boil while she spoons the carrot between Angela's lips, feeling the strange new tink of teeth on the metal spoon.

Then they fight. Derek and Lin have a fight. It is about Christmas. He who is Jewish and an atheist does not want to celebrate Christmas. She who is nothing is particular suddenly does. Voices are raised. Lin slams down Angela's spoon, causing the egg cup to tip over and the still-soft white to spill. She kicks off her slippers, stamps into her boots, storms out the front door — but

rushing down the snowy steps to the car she is followed by Angela's cries

she jabs the key into the ignition, makes the motor howl with rage

then turns it off; she is not allowed to do this anymore

Derek has slipped his arms around her from behind and now his tongue is following the soft ridges of her left ear downward and inward, Lin sinks to sit on the bed, twisting her body at the same time to face her husband's, grasping him hard by the hips she crushes eyes, nose, mouth to his trousers

and feels him harden through the layers of cloth, her scalp
and fingertips and nipples tingle

she holds his sex between her two hands and delicately
circles with her tongue its fragile ring of flesh, then parts
her lips

his hands grip her hair, pulling it, for balance and to stave
off the waves of pleasure, there are tears in her eyes, she is
filled with him, his nails dig into her shoulders, it lasts, lasts,
and then he bellows and comes, bellows again, again, his
body collapses on top of hers.

The cry — the slight cry — and Lin is up, moving with
eyes half closed, barefoot, swiftly. The slight cry again — and
already she is bending over her daughter's crib.

The touch of her hand on the child's head is the touch of
a wand — Angela goes back to sleep.

Lin drives three hours west with Angela in her basket
on the backseat. She has brought daffodils from their garden
for Bess.

The neighborhood and then the house are as dismal as
she remembers. How can people have neon lights in their
kitchens? Even Angela looks blotched and ugly in this light.
Where's Dad? Lin asks Bess, glancing around.

He just stepped out to get a few six-packs, her stepmother says.
Maybe I'll take Angela for a walk while we wait for Gramps
to get back.

But you just got here, Bess protests.

I know, says Lin, planting a kiss on her soft and flabby cheek. But I feel a little woozy from the drive.

She rolls the stroller to the end of the block, staring at her daughter's feet in their pink slippers. Right now today, she thinks, your feet are just precisely the length of my middle finger.

Above them float the sounds of a mother and son who are spending the day in a shoddy small apartment. The son emits irritated little yelps. The mother mimics them sarcastically. The son cries in outrage. The mother gives him a resounding slap on the face. The son screams. There is a brief moment of silence. Then the mother begins to sing to her little boy in Portuguese. Lin gets hastily to her feet and pushes the stroller away from this scene of milk and murder.

Her father's belly has swollen to thrice its former size and his black-grimed hands shake a little. Lin notices he cannot look at her directly. The conversation is frighteningly foggy, vague complaints about the garage owner's back payments on electricity that get bogged down in a tussle between January and February. Wordlessly, generously, Bess dishes out macaroni and cheese on plastic plates, then washes up while they are still at table. Lin feels Angela being slowly tainted by the haze of beer and smoke and ordinariness.

She phones Derek from Bess's chintzy bedroom and — on the pretext of some minor emergency at home — they leave later the same day.

Driving eastward, Lin rages inwardly against reality. The

tiredness now around Bess's eyes. The desperate way in which she eats, cramming food into herself as if to stop up some enormous inner gap. Poor Bess — she's worried about the way my father has been drinking since he retired. She's given him so much, been so absolutely loyal.

Why don't people grow beautiful instead of ugly as they age?

Sheer, bare, arbitrary reality.

Essence only flutters there.

Do you know where my mommy is? Angela asks the museum attendant.

Sure, she's right over there he says, pointing at Lin.

Angela runs across the room and joyfully buries her face in Lin's skirt. Then she goes back to the attendant. Do you know where my mommy is?

Sure, she's right over there.

Angela runs across the room and joyfully buries her face in Lin's skirt. Then she goes back to the attendant. Do you know were my mommy is?

Sure, she's right over there.

Angela runs across the room and joyfully buries her face in Lin's skirt.

Do you know where my mommy is?

Lin knows that her mother's name was Marilyn and that she was a runaway. She had fled home at age seventeen because her parents bashed her regularly over the head with frying pans and golf clubs and hunting rifles. She had stolen a car though she barely knew how to drive, driven east until the car ran out of gas, then hitchhiked with the gas can to the nearest town and looked around for a service station. Joe, who happened to be working the pumps that day, had been struck by her wild eyes. Two weeks later she was pregnant and four years later she was dead. She was blond. She and Joe had been in love.

This is all Lin knows.

She has never tried to find her maternal grandparents, whom she holds responsible for the hemorrhage of Marilyn's twenty-one-year-old brain.

Angela goes up the staircase, counting the steps under her breath.

Two, seven, two, seven, two, seven, two, seven.

They are in bed, at midnight.

This morning, Lin says to Derek, I taught Angela how to put on her socks. I told her look, you put the heels of the sock down here on the bottom, see? Because that's where the heels of your feet are. If you put it on the other way around, there'll be a big empty pocket up here for nothing, see?

Derek laughs.

It's not funny at all, says Lin. She's left us, as far as putting on socks is concerned.

There are three things to be ascertained about each and every object: is it alive, can it talk, can we pet it.

Hey, stop fooling around with my cock.

I'm just petting it. Can it talk?

What's that?

A garter snake.

Can it talk?

No, it's dead.

And when it's alive can it talk?

Nope.

Can we pet it?

Am I gonna die, Mommy?
Yup. Everybody's going to die.
We won't be able to talk anymore?
Nope. We won't be able to do anything. But don't worry, it won't happen for a long time yet.
Now we can talk?
Yes, because now we're alive.
And are *you* gonna die, Mommy?

A wonderful play on which the curtain is bound to fall.

Butchered by a backroom abortionist as a teenager, Bess could not have children. Dear Bess, forgive me. I was never able to call you Mommy. I know you did your best.

I must have called my mother Mommy, though. If she died when I was three I must have called her Mommy a thousand times.

It was Bess who had been the unwitting instrument of Lin's revelation — by taking her to a puppet show when she was four. That rainy Saturday afternoon had changed her life. The flood of relief — so there *was* another world! So one *wasn't* condemned to live in this one all the time!

Don't touch Mommy's things, Lin overhears Derek telling Angela.

Then it is actually true. Even when she is not there, she is still Mommy to Angela. It is absolutely real, not a play at all.

Why do little girls giggle and whisper all the time? Lin asks
Rachel. Is it hormonal, do you think?
Beats me, says Rachel.
   Lin lowers her voice to a whisper.
Do you think cavegirls used to giggle and whisper too?
   They giggle.

Come on, let's go take a bath, says Derek.
No, I don't want to.
Come on, it'll be a really nice bath.
Okay.
Okay?
I'll just take the nice but I don't want the bath.

From the kitchen Lin can hear Derek mock wailing Stop it, Daddy! You're getting soap in my eyes! so that Angela will laugh instead of cry as he rinses her hair

Darkness surrounds the house. Lin sautés the lamb, attentive to the way the meat hisses as it sticks to the pot and then is prodded away with the wooden spoon, turns on its red side, brown and blackens and hisses, spattering hot grease. The smell fills the kitchen. Lin sweeps garlic peels into the garbage can and suddenly, staring at it, begins to elicit every particle of its contents: congealed grease, coffee grounds, tin cans, pink-smeared yogurt containers, dirty diapers — ah the rich filth of it, the pithy mulch of it, the garbage memories, back alleys in New York, gaunt figures rummaging through wastebaskets in Central Park, six o'clock clang bang of trash cans being hurled into trucks and mashed by revolving teeth, mountains of mangled cars in New Jersey — all of it, all of it, she wants it all.

Angela on her father's back, ineffably lovely in her pink terry-cloth bathrobe, cheeks red from the hot bath, hair damp and curling tightly.

Derek is feeding Angela ground beef and green peas. Lin watches her husband's lips turn into motorcycles and motorboats, swooping planes and chugging trains — each spoonful a different vehicle returning to garage or hangar or port. Who would have expected a staid Spinoza specialist to have such thespian talent?

Angela take the spoon from her father, fills it with food and says Airplane, imitating the noise of a jumbo jet as she brings it toward her face — but at the last second her left hand darts up and covers her mouth, the spoon crashes into it and the food goes flying in all directions

Stay here with me, Mommy.
I can't honey, we've got company.
If you don't stay I'm gonna have a bad dream.
Try to think about nice things before you go to sleep, that way you'll have nice dreams.
I'm thinking about not-nice things. I'm thinking about dead turtles . . . and dead butterflies . . . and coats — coats aren't nice . . . and cupboards — cupboards aren't nice . . .
Good night, darling.

Fire glints off whiskey glasses and earrings and watches, the intellectuals are standing there and talking and nodding, creatures so used to feigning poise that these odd angular postures, thumb hooked round belt loop or wrist planted on hip, have become second nature to them.
What will you have to drink? Derek is asking someone.

Straight vodka, the man says.

I'll have straight orange juice, please — a female voice.

Fine, fine, chortles the man. That way you get the screw and I get the driver.

Lin knows she will remain mute as they wend their way through the evening's conversation, discussing tenure and calories and cholesterol, the politics of this country, the films they have recently seen or read about, who among them has quit smoking and who has started up again — and Rachel is off lecturing somewhere; there is not even Rachel to joke with in the kitchen, to make fun of the others with, to wink at across the table.

But during the meal there is a man who unexpectedly joins her in her silence, keeps her company by not speaking, a man she has never seen before but whose eyes, deep wells of pain and irony, keep entering hers and agreeing with her wish that they be suddenly elsewhere, the two of them, together, and as the conversation plods through its mandatory stations of the cross she starts to fall in love with these eyes. She scarcely touches the lamb stew and when she looks at Derek he seems to her a typically bland academic with glasses and glib tongue, whereas their silence, Lin's and this stranger's silence, is full and pulsates with dark promise — they raise their glasses — Drink to me only — they are making love together, there at the table — she is saying yes and yes and yes and he is pulling away her clothes and moving onto her and entering her gently swollen and trembling and moving slowly there until she is on the verge of implosion —

yes still she has not withdrawn her eyes from his and now she
almost weeps with the want of him.

   Later she is setting coffee cups and saucers on a tray and
he comes to join her in the kitchen, now she cannot raise
her eyes to his; dry-mouthed and with half a smile she says I
didn't catch your name — and he, his back turned to the
doorway through which anyone might come at any moment,
strokes her check with one finger and says Sean Farrell, Sean
Farrell, over and over, as though it were her name instead of
his, his finger drawing a slow straight line down her jaw
down her neck down over her collarbone and chest, ending at
her nipple — then he whispers, conspiratorially
You hate academic dinners, don't you?

   She nods.

A university, you know, is nothing but a shattered universe.
Each scholar has one little, brittle shard of it inside his head,
and nothing else.

And which particular shard have you in yours? Lin asks. Bur
Sean lays his finger on her lips, then moves his own lips
toward her until they brush his finger.

   In the dining room again he is relaxed; his silence has
grown expansive and he smiles at her as if they had already
become lovers, as if the warm solid secret of their shared bodies protected them from all the intellectual inanity. He does
not take coffee but finishes, alone, the remaining half bottle
of wine.

The most interesting thing I heard all evening, Lin says afterward to Derek, was Cupboards aren't nice.
Who said that?
Angela.
   And later,
Who's Sean Farrell?
A poet with a gift for instilling discomfort. Prying a knife edge under the soft blue folds of literary cloth. Dispelling romantic haze. That sort of thing.
I see. He scarcely opened his mouth all evening. Except to imbibe.
Did you ever hear of an Irish Poet who wasn't an alcoholic?

   The next morning, Sunday, Angela wakens them at dawn, crawling into bed with them.
   Lin warms milk for her on the stove downstairs. A dramatic deep-pink slit in the sky, beyond the fine black latticework of winter trees, slices the smudge of cloud at the horizon. Back between the musky morning sheets her husband's body is hot to her cool limbs. Angela holds the bottle with one hand, tips back her head and drinks with great singleness of purpose, drawing strong regular spurts of tepid chocolate milk from the bottle
   what was it like to nurse her
   Derek enters her from behind. A moan and Angela turns her head. Lin bites her lips, smiles at her daughter, slides with excruciating slowness down her husband's hard still cock.

Then she closes her eyes and Sean is there too, his finger running down her cheek and neck to her nipple, and the pleasure shoves her under. Angela's coos and gurgles come from very far away. Derek is above Lin now, still behind her, laboring her, no longer careful about his heavy rasping gasps, no she does not want Angela to see their bodies joined this way, the strain and distortion of their features, but it is all right, Angela is banging her bottle gaily on the bedside table and when her father explodes into her mother she doesn't miss a beat.

And she pricked her finger on the spinning wheel and fell into a deep, deep sleep. The time has come, the walrus said, to speak of many things. I'll huff and I'll puff and I'll blow your house down. Hang your clothes on the hickory bush, but don't go near the water. And this was scarcely odd because they'd eaten every one. How much wood would a woodchuck chuck if a woodchuck could chuck wood? The goblins will get you if you don't watch out!

So you see, the first little pig, he built his house all out of straw. And then this nice little wolf came along and knocked very gently on this door. Knock, knock, knock. Who's there? It's the wolf, can I come in? Not by the hair of my chinny-chin-chin. But I don't want to eat you, I just want to be friends.

Angela lapses into silence.
Then what happens?
I don't know . . .
Lin laughs and hugs and rocks her daughter and laughs.

My little girl just started singing, Nijinsky had scribbled in his secret notebook. *She is going "Ah, ah, ah." Whatever can that mean? I have the feeling that for her it means, "Ah, ah! nothing is horrible — all is joy!"*

Lin is sleeping badly these days, as always when a new dance is inside her. Her body throws obstacles in her path as if she didn't want or weren't allowed to do it. She battles with neck aches and screaming knees, head colds and twisted ankles, the way fairy-tale heroines fight to overcome combs that shoot up into forests and scarves that lengthen into rushing rivers.

She grits her teeth. She pads her knees and ankles and elbows and wrists, layer upon layer of warmth and protection, until the person she sees in her wall of mirrors ludicrously resembles a rugby player.

They are standing on the bridge. There is snow on either bank, but the river isn't frozen over yet. Angela is dropping sticks and stones into the water. The pebbled path leading to the bridge is a spilled treasure chest. How does she know which pebbles to choose?
Why do all children love throwing stones into the water? Lin asks Derek.
What do you mean, why? It's wonderful, isn't it?
Lin thinks it over. Yes, it is wonderful, she says to herself finally.
Please don't climb up on the bridge, sweetheart, you're scaring me.
Are you afraid I'm gonna drown?
Yes.
Why don't you want me to be dead?
Because you're the only little girl I've got.
You could have another one!
Yes, but you're my only Angela.
You could call her Angela . . . Are you afraid her hair won't be as blond as mine?

At the playground, now that Angela can run and jump and swing, the babies in their carriages and strollers look like passive bland rag dolls.

Eyes closed, Lin is a puppet and each of Emile's drum-beats is a tug on one of her strings. Her body is jerked to and fro by the rhythm — steady in the left hand, erratic in the right — and there is nothing she can do to stop it. She is manipulated, yanked, bending as if punched in the stomach when the deep thumps resound again and again, executing footwork so complex it would be impossible without the relentless rhythm that compels her.

This lasts more than an hour. When they stop, although steaming with sweat, Lin is untired.

I don't know where I went, she says. But I sure wasn't here anymore.

I know, nods Emile. Ever since I was a kid I've thought that's what bowing meant — effacing yourself. It wasn't me, it was beauty. I don't exist, all the credit goes to beauty. Just the opposite of a boxing champion waving his fat gloves in the air.

They sit there in silence.

My turn at the drum, says Lin at last.

Now she has the cylinder between her thighs, its tight smooth skin beneath her fingers. She taps softly, watches Emile's body like a twisting melting candle with its flame of hair and tries to capture it with her fingertips. Yes now she has it, now it is hers. She slaps hard, the body arches — yes. They are off. She makes the drumbeat sensuous then violent, monotonous then syncopated, relishing the instantaneous results of her playing in Emile's hips and shoulders. She forces him to toss his head, bend backward slowly, throw himself from side to side, stretch out his arms for mercy. The two of them are welded together by the throbbing air.

Suddenly Lin's hands allow a silence to dive into the middle of her playing — it lands with a thud and Emile's body is thrown off balance, he spins to catch himself, then follows the cascade of drumbeats as they decrescendo to the floor. Lin has laid him down. Silence arrives like a blanket to cover him.

After the dress rehearsal she descends glowing streaming from the stage and is brought up short. Sean Farrell is seated in the front row, his eyes are on her, his eyes have been following her body for the past two hours and she didn't know, never in all their years together has Derek attended one of her rehearsals Will you have a drink with me, do you have time? he says, without smiling, as she shakes his hand.

In the bar they proffer cursory information about themselves. Lin learns that Sean's background is poor, Catholic and harsh; that he was nine years old when his father died; that he loves his mother with a desperation born of pity.

He stirs his second martini in silence. Lights a cigarette and takes three or four deep drags. She waits, her glass of mineral water untouched on the table in front of her. She wonders whether he can read the beating of her heart on her temples. *What* are you doing? Sean says finally. His voice is low but dark, almost threatening. When you have that in your body. *How* can you go on playing the professor's wife in a piddly little college town — don't you know your gift will be throttled here? You might as well take up crocheting right away and have done with it.

A wave of cold has traveled across Lin's scalp from the top of her forehead to the nape of her neck. Whereas *your* gift, I gather, simply thrives on backwoods provincialism, she says, so breathless with rage her voice is scarcely audible.

I wanted to talk about *you. To you.*

Sean crushes his cigarette in the ashtray and takes Lin's freezing hand in his two warm hands.

She jerks it away from him, rises stiffly, stalks out of the bar.

They have said the words Let's make another child. Do you want a son this time? says Lin.

I don't give a hoot in hell, says Derek. I just want more of what we've already got. More potties in the bathroom and more plastic ducks in the bathtub and more boxes of Honey-smacks spilled all over the kitchen floor.

They are standing in their bedroom fully dressed, she with her back to him, and as Angela sleeps her snoring sleep in the next room the mere idea of making another child is enough to bring the sweat to their skins. Derek kneels behind her and lowers her black tights to her thighs, touches her with tongue and fingers until she is drenched and quaking, then drags her white shift up over her shoulders and head and off her but leaves the tights as they are and, jerking her arm up behind her back, ripping open his trousers, enters her deeply, more and more deeply, until — keening, whining, whinnying —

She is trembling, trembling, doubled over with pain. Always it is the same thing.

It's all right, Emile tells her reassuringly. You'll be all right.

I know, says Lin with a shamefaced grin.

She cannot walk. Her body, muscles cramped, tendons shrieking, is one bunched knot of pain. She cannot walk and in five minutes she must dance.

Emile puts his arm around her. Just the contact of his skin on hers is enough to make her want to scream — she will die, she is sure of it, her body will be torn to shreds by the thorns and prickles before she reaches the enchanted heart of the forest — oh no, this time she'll never make it —

The house is packed. The thousand faint murmurs and rustles and coughs of the audience merge into an ominous hum that can only grow and grow and grow until it engulfs her.

Black. The hum diminishes and dies.

Emile has vanished. Then she sees him, his red hair burnished copper by the spotlight. He is up there, his hands already stroking the warm skin of the drum.

And the beat comes, calling her.

As she moves onto the stage the pain falls away from her, shed like a mantle, and she emerges from it tall and invulnerable. An invisible flame licks the soles of her bare feet and courses through her, warming without burning. The silence in the hall is absolute, nothing can move now, apart from her, not a muscle can twitch, not an eyelash bat without her permission. Lin is huge, gorgeously huge, and she commands the vast rectangle of the stage which is the universe. Her body

is a brain which grasps all, encompasses all, controls all . . .
She will teach them. She will shower them with beauty.

When her arm describes an arc in the air it is not an arm,
it is the sunrise; when her head drops floorward it is not a
head but the thundering of boulders down a mountainside;
when her foot skids sideways it is not a foot, it is hunger and
sarcasm, cruelly dashed hopes.

She scarcely feels the splinter of pinewood that has
shoved itself deep into her heel. Its presence too, instanta-
neously, is made part of the dance.

But the minute she leaves the stage, pain shoots through
her from foot to brain. It was waiting for her backstage,
impatient to pounce on her. She doubles over, covering her
mouth with both hands.

Emile extracts the splinter with tweezers, whistling
under his breath. It is fully two inches long.
Your turn at the drums, he says.

Sean Farrell attends every single one of her perform-
ances. When she bows at the end, she sees that he is not clap-
ping but staring at her with the utmost earnestness. And
often, leaving the theater arm in arm with Emile, she catches
sight of him hovering in the shadows, smoking a cigarette,
watching her.

She reads the thin volume of his poetry Derek owns. It
disturbs her.

Then he begins to send her letters. All the letter say the
same thing. I know you. I love you, but that does not matter.

What matters is that your place is not here.

She longs to kiss him. She longs to kill him. His eyes wake her at night and his poems throb beneath her skin.

One day, window-shopping on Main Street with Rachel, she runs into him. Realizes she has never seen him before in broad daylight, and that she knows him better than Derek. Blushes to the roots of her hair when her stupid heart starts thumping away. Blurts out the introductions

but Rachel and Sean are already shaking hands; they are staring at each other and a thousand sparklers have suddenly caught fire between their bodies, an aura of electricity surrounds them

Of course, thinks Lin, fairly leaping backward to avoid the shock, Rachel and Sean, of course.

Good night, my darling.

Don't go away, Mommy.

Why not?

Because as soon as you go, my . . . my . . .

Your instructors come?

Yes.

And what do they do to you?

They make me clean up.

You have to clean up the house?

No.

The city?

No.

What, then?

The sky. I have to clean all the clouds or else they'll catch me.

And what'll they do to you if they catch you?
They'll bash my head in! They'll kick me! They'll stick knives in my eyes!
But Angela! No one has the right to kick you around! You tell them if they do that, we'll come and kick *them* around, okay?
But you can't see them! Unless . . . I've got some pink powder in my pockets, it's magic . . . Maybe . . .

The tug at the base of her stomach. She is certain.

The new child's heartbeat amplified tap-tap, tap-tap by the microphone.
That's the conductor's beat for the entire symphony of your pregnancy, Lin's doctor tells her.
Lin beams.
It won't stop until this person dies, do you realize that? she says to Derek.

With Angela, pregnancy had been like nine months of orgasm — a perpetual stimulation of that burning center of the dance, the long vibrating cone from sex to throat. And to think that a *person* was being manufactured in there! To think that, as she went about her daily life, her body was patiently weaving tissues and stacking cells, organizing another human entity — never had Lin experienced such a sense of wonder.
This second baby weighs more, moves more, hurts more

than the first. It hiccups violently inside her every evening after dinner.

That kid is blind drunk, says Derek. I bet it can't even walk a straight line.

With Angela, Lin had been able to dance until seven months — ah! like Twyla, wonderful Twyla Tharp and her *Family Dance,* the body lurching drunkenly back, forth, left, right, losing and rediscovering balance, reinventing balance — but this time she is impeded as of four. Warmups make her dizzy and red in the face; and as soon as she tries to leap, her stomach turns to cement.

Then one day she loses some blood. Horrified, she cancels all classes and engagements. Stops dancing completely.

I'm gonna have thousands of children, says Angela. I'm gonna have fourteen! I'm gonna have ELEVEN! I'll put two Kleenexes at once in my 'gina and that way I'll have twins! Two Tampaxes, you mean?
Yeah.

Bess demonstrating on her own body how sanitary napkins were attached by pinning one to the outside of her black ski pants, first up in front over her fat belly, then up in back over her fat behind. Dear Bess, she always meant well. She didn't intend to be absurd. No one is tacky and tasteless on purpose. But I didn't want my friends to meet her and mistake her, God forbid, for my real mother

no, my real mother was blond and blithe and beautiful
an elf, a sprite
the sparkle of light on water
everything that shimmered, everything that danced was
my mother

With Angela in her stomach, making love had been
insanely blissful for both of them. They could not get over it.
They could not get enough of it. Longer and more lan-
guorously than ever before, they had reveled in the sheer
swoon of sex.
My God, you'll drown the baby if you keep this up, she had
told Derek once, overflowing with his semen.
This time, encumbered, she prefers to caress herself
alone, during the day. Clothes make her uncomfortable, the
material scratches and inflames her skin, zippers and elastics
leave angry red marks.
Sometimes in her dance room she strips naked and
stands there staring at her bulbous body in the wall of mirrors. Time stops. She folds her hands between her leaking
breasts and nothing happens. She is there and that is all.
Dance this: the body as matter to be moved. Stuttering
stubborn substance.

The pains are atrocious from the start.
Are you having the *concracktions?* says Angela.
I sure am.

On the way to the clinic she jokes with Derek about Martha Graham's dancers, trained to the point of obsession in contract-release but notoriously bad at giving birth. Then she stops joking, stops talking

there are no words for how serious the pain is

it seems intent on murdering her, there are no words

it's one or the other, she keeps thinking, one or the other

Again it is a girl. They call her Marina, because of the Russian poetess. She is hefty and fierce looking. A howler.

Angela is taken aback.

Marina is two weeks old. Oh to look and look and look and look at you, do nothing but register the million fleeting movements of your face, your pursed lips and lopsided smile, your rolling eyeballs and hunger gape, the gradual screwing up and reddening of your features when you shit, your open-mouthed tearless cries of sometimes hunger, sometimes not.

Her tiny pointed tongue is so tiny and so pointed, the fuzz on her smooth head is so fuzzy, the soft skin of her fingers so unbelievably soft. Her hands gesticulate with astonishing eloquence, whereas her eyes still swivel and cross comically in their sockets and her bum still emits the most innocent of farts.

Marina cries and cries. She screams until her entire body shakes. No gaze, no smile, no caress Lin can bestow on her is of any avail, for it is Lin who makes her cry. Marina's appetite is stirred by the odor of her mother's body, which drips from morning to night with blood and milk and sweat — whereas in Derek's firm dry arms she can forget about food and fall asleep.

At night, Lin dreams she is playing with Marina. Suddenly she hears a baby screaming and is relieved to be able to tell herself, That's not my baby, that baby has nothing to do with me, it's not my responsibility, I don't have to look after it, I can just go on playing with my little girl . . . Meanwhile the real Marina is screaming, screaming.

Derek! Come and see! Marina turned over all by herself!

Already Marina's childhood is erasing Angela's. How shall I love them, where can I keep this, what can be saved?

The ugly dawns, yes the stark bleak dawns of winter. Pacing with Marina as the world sleeps and the sky whitens, no sap no greenness or vibrancy anywhere. Five in the February morning, holding this baby wrapped in a patchwork quilt, rocking with it in the dark, going nowhere but back and forth, back and forth, staring dully at the final crimson embers of last night's fire.

How to recover this, how to use it for the dance — always Lin's work, her love, her passion has been to take life's darkest themes and turn them into light, not edulcorating but magnifying them, freezing their fleeting forms and allowing them to crystallize, then bursting them back into movement — nothing must exist that cannot be folded into the body and there transfigured.

Lin rocks and rocks, the tears running down her face.

When Marina finally drops off, Lin does not trust her sleep as she trusted Angela's — she does not believe in it, it does not reassure her.

She's driving me crazy, Lin declares at last.

Why don't you wean her, Derek suggest gently.

But this too — the fact that her mother no longer smells of sweet milk, no longer offers her nipples of warm flesh, only nipples of cold rubber — enrages Marina.

For Lin it is better, though. Now each morning she can kiss her children good-bye.

She resumes rehearsing with a vengeance. She has been asked to perform in New York and there is a new duo in her brain, struggling to get out. It scares her even more than usual. It is about stone and sculpture, about failure leading to rage, then madness and finally to imprisonment. But first she must learn to turn air into stone and sculpt it, chisel it patiently, bring out the shapes it secretly contains.

This will be her most powerful piece to date, she is sure of it — but she needs to go so very far away

Marina's first word is Byebye. Before Mommy, before Daddy, before Cookie: Byebye.

We'll explain to them later about politics and suffering, right? says Lin.

Right, says Derek.

For the time being we can just keep teaching them how to spread jam on their toast, right?

Right.

We can't expect them to learn everything at once, right? Right says Derek. And we'll never tell them, Boy you're just a couple of spoiled brats, you don't realize what a cushy life you've got, we never had it so good when we were kids, we got up at the crack of dawn, ate nothing but cold porridge, did backbreaking chores around the house and started earning our own living in a coal mine at the age of eight.

Right, says Lin.

Emile won't be here to work with her on the new duo until eleven.

As she warms up in her dance room flooded with sunlight, Lin hears a subdued roar coming from downstairs — Theresa doing the vacuuming. Dancing, she follows the vacuum cleaner in her mind's eye from the kitchen to hall to living room, noses with it beneath the sofa, slides with it across the Turkish rug, knocks with it into hardwood corners, sucks up with it the dust and hair and particles of grit shed by her family

dust to dust
I shall love thee unto the grave

Isadora too had danced in public with a baby boy swimming in her stomach, surfing her waves. She had been taught to dance by the Pacific Ocean, racing as a child along its edge, following the rise and fall of the breakers, imitating their running without rush, and look what happened look what happened look what happened, one afternoon she kissed her two children good-bye and ten minutes later the car with Patrick and Deirdre and their nurse in the backseat went rolling down the embankment into the Seine, rolling down the embankment into the Seine, the water rose and rose, the car sank and sank, and the children flailed and choked as the water rushed into their lungs, filling them completely so that the children were weightless at last, freed at last from the demands of gravity — No I do not want this, said Isadora, I did not want these dead children, I cannot bear them again, *how shall I ever dance again, how stretch out my arms except in desolation?* No no no no, she said, the only life there is, is *up where the spirit can fly — freed of this abominable bad dream of matter . . . I know that all these so-called happenings are illusions, she said — Water cannot drown people, neither can going without food starve them, neither are they born or do they die — ALL IS*

the baby Deirdre was an illusion after all, she was not born and she has not died

What have I done, thinks Lin
oh my God what have I done
The dance already so fragile, so dependent, dying each and every second as it is born; the dance already the mortal child of my mortal body but now these girls as well, now these clamoring clambering girls, what have I done

Emile arrives and Lin continues to see the little weightless corpses bobbing about inside the car, their hair lifting away from their scalps and waving in the water like seaweed — No you may not bury them, said Isadora, never will they enter the earth! No more earth — no more water — nothing but fire and air! Let the children be cremated! let their tiny limp bodies turn into flame, ash, smoke! let them rise and float away into the air!

What's the matter, Lin? asks Emile.
I'm sorry. Can we take it again?

Dust to dust. Earth to earth. I will love thee unto the grave.

Must come down to earth. Must grovel. Must learn all there is to know about mud, the here, the now, must learn to love the heaviness and smirch. Or else.

Derek. I want to let Theresa go.
What? What for?
Lin takes a deep breath.
I'd rather do the housework myself.

Blinding brilliant snow heaps in the sun, and the calligraphy of black branches against the blue wash of the sky. Why does the first browning and falling of their leaves always fill me with foreboding? wonders Lin. Trees in summer are so blatant and bombastic by comparison with their still and skeletal winter selves . . .

She slides the iron's hot point beneath the arm of one of Angela's T-shirts, a pink one with a regular scattering of small white flowers, presses, smooths downward, lifts the iron, moves up to the other side, repeats.

Best of all is reaching into the dryer, dragging out armfuls of warm dry clothes and carrying them — gently so as not to crush them — to the kitchen table, then sorting them, making tight rolls of little colored socks, folding diminutive panties with lace at the waist or cartoon characters on the stomach.

Marina hates for Lin to answer the telephone.

Not hello! *Not* hello! she says angrily.

She especially hates for Lin to go out in the evenings.

But honey, I have a rehearsal. You know I can't be here just every single night.

Me too, I'm coming to the hersal.

No darling, you can't. It's going to last until the middle of the night. You go to bed at seven and Mommy won't be finished until — counting on her fingers — eight, nine, ten, eleven, TWELVE! But we can take a bath together if you want, before I leave. If you promise not to get my hair wet.

I promise.

Marina fills her plastic boat with water and pours it directly onto her mother's head. Unlaughlingly. It is not even a joke, not even a mistake.

Angela wants to start ballet lessons. Why not? So every Wednesday: minute pink leotards and slippers, taffeta tutu, hair twisted into ponytail and barrettes clipped to temples

Mothers watching their pint-and-white daughters with their flat stretched stomachs and twig legs, as they leap and spring and hesitate, turn the wrong way, blush and blink and curtsey. All of them are dainty and white skinned and well fed

Well I'm not going to teach her. Well I can't teach her. The dance is not something that can pass from me to a child of mine.

Angela in Lin's dance room. Admiring herself in the glass. Blowing kisses to the imaginary audience. Curtseying to the applause in her head.

She wants to be like me. She wants to be me.

Can I have some cold cream, too?
Sure.
Can I have some more?
Okay, but just a little.
    Angela plunges her whole hand into the Nivea jar. Hey! she says. Your Mommy told you to take a *little!* Yeah I know, but I wanted to take *a lot!* Why? *Because,* that's why!

Angela comes to the dinner table with bright red dots of lipstick on her cheeks.

Look, Derek, says Lin. Our daughter must have been out picking cherries today.

At bedtime, Angela says, You know, Mommy, when you made fun of me because I had cherries on my cheeks, my heart cried and its heart was broken. And then my heart's heart cried, and *its* heart was broken. And the same for all my hearts, all the way to my back.

Mommy, Mommy, Mommy, I like your name better than mine, I want to trade names with you *right now*, please say yes. But sweetheart, Daddy and I called you Angela because we thought it was the nicest name in the world.

Yeah, but we can have different tastes — you know, like your favorite color is blue and mine is pink and I don't like my name very much but I think your name is the most beautiful name in the whole world and I want to be called Lin Lhomond, please say yes, *please! Please!* okay?

Aren't you worried people will mistake you for the famous dancer? jokes Lin.

Ha! They'll be pretty surprised, won't they? For such a little girl to be so famous — oh please, Mommy! If you say no I'll hit myself in the eye, I'll take a nail and hammer it into my eye —

Angela! Stop it!

Stop it. Right this minute. Do you hear me? If you don't

do this, I'll do that. If you do this, I'll give you that. Come here before I lose my temper. I'll count to five. The way intelligent women turn into stupid mothers.

Dance this?

They try with Marina all the tricks that worked with Angela, and they do not work.

When Marina stubs her toe on a kitchen chair or hangs her head on the corner of a table and starts to screech, Derek strides over to the guilty piece of furniture and demands, hand on hips, How dare you hurt my little girl, you mean old table, you? He gives it a fake kick, then grabs his foot and hops around the room — Ow, ow, it hurt me too! — but Marina, instead of laughing, screeches even louder

At table, no metamorphosis into helicopter, motorcycle, rocketship, butterfly or hummingbird can persuade Marina to swallow a spoonful of food she has decided not to swallow.

In the bathtub, Let-me-cry-instead-of-you holds no water whatsoever. No matter how carefully and playfully they go about washing her hair, Marina screams so stridently that their eardrums throb.

Derek has flown far away, he is in a desert somewhere talking about ethics. And Angela is visiting her grandparents, Sidney and Violet, in New Jersey. So Lin finds herself alone with Marina for an entire weekend.

It is past midnight but Lin cannot sleep therefore Marina cannot sleep therefore Lin cannot sleep therefore Marina cannot sleep. Her dry desolate cry stirs her mother's guts like a wooden spoon, scrapes her skin like a knife. *Why* is she crying like this, what does she know about me.

Later it is Lin who wakes and shakes, stomach churning, mouth flooded with saliva — there are dark flappings like crows' wings at the edges of her brain, grimy strings trailing across the screen — who is making whom sick? she wonders. Who started this? And how will it ever end?

Don't you dare wake me up again, she says, the fourth time Marina's wails drag her from her bed. But Marina begins to cry the instant her mother's hands release her body.

Let her cry!

Let them cry half an hour, says Doctor Spock.

Barefoot, Lin descends to the kitchen, closes the door and turns on the radio, picks up a magazine and fills herself with peanuts and words and music and alcohol so that her daughter's screams may not enter her. When finally she re-emerges from the kitchen, drunk and nauseous, there is silence on the second floor.

But Marina wakes again at seven. It is Sunday, rain slants heavily out of a slate sky, the town will be closed all day like a fist and they won't be able to go out for a walk.

Marina refuses to let her read or rehearse, so Lin throws herself into the filthiest jobs she can think of.

She cleans the oven. No one has done this since Theresa left. Months of accrued grease and meat juices and over-flowed pie fillings and sticky burnt fruit. The ammonia fumes of the cleaning product sear her nostrils, inflame her throat.

Then she polishes every shoe and boot in the house, excavating them from second-floor closets and abandoned trunks. Black polish, brown polish, white polish, beige. Rub scrub spic span shine.

When Marina yells for lunch, it is still only eleven-thirty.

Mercifully, in the afternoon she naps. Lin enters Derek's study and stares at his empty desk. Then she pulls Marina's baby album down from a high shelf.

There she is, there she is, the camera says so.

Marina, Marina.

The house shudders under the weight of the sky's tears.

Marina wails. Lin huddles in the corner of a couch with her, stroking her hair. They must hold out until six o'clock, when Derek will be home. No one is crazy here, no one is crazy

Look sweetheart, says Derek. The sun is going to bed.

Yeah, says Marina. And don't you *dare* wake up in the middle of the night, sun!

Mommy, says Angela, if you died —
I'd want you to burn my body.
No! I'd bury you right here in the living room. No, I'd keep your body with me forever. I'd burn my cheek so I could die and be buried right next to you. I'd take all your dresses and all your clothes, they're so pretty. I'd cut all your hair off and make myself a wig.

It is late afternoon dark and Lin is alone, about to begin slicing onions. Then a cricket is in the corner of her eye, scraping slowly across the living-room floor.

She removes her slipper and swats it
returns to the kitchen for a dustpan
dumps the cricket onto the fire

But the insect is revived by the heat to endure a far crueler death. Lin stands there, hypnotized. It was dead but now it is moving, flailing, waving its legs faster and faster, then more and more slowly as gradually its body cooks. Finally it dissolves with a hiss into the glow.

my children can die

At first Isadora could not weep and then she wept and then she traveled to a war-wracked country and worked ceaselessly, selflessly to help children who were starving, but her pain did not diminish so she went to Italy and hid in the house of a friend and went for long solitary walks along the beach, but still her pain endured, still it yawned and roared and threatened to engulf her

and then

late one evening next to the lapping waves of the Adriatic she saw — yes, with her own eyes saw

her two children, more than a year dead

there, in the flesh

but when she ran to throw her arms around them

they dissolved into nothingness

and Isadora slumped to the ground, clutching gritty wet sand to her soft breasts, lips, stomach

then suddenly a young Italian man materialized out of nowhere, laid a hand on her shoulder and said,
Can I help you?
Oh yes, she said, help me please! Give me a child.

So he went with her to the home of her friend, he poured his seed into her and a child began to grow inside of her; Isadora knew it was a male child and she returned to Paris believing she would dance again. But when, ripe and nine months formed, the male child decided to try its luck on the earth, along came August 1914 and Paris was so tickled to be sending its young men off to war that it was impossible to get a bottle of oxygen to this incipient young man in time and he died too

Rachel on the telephone.

Lin, I'm hopelessly in love. Sean is my twin brother. He loves me from my toenails to my parietal lobe. I've never laughed so much in my life!

Lin is spying on her children. Standing at the high window of her dance room, she stealthily parts the white tulle curtains an inch or two and watches Angela and Marina playing together in the sandbox.

These are her daughters' bodies. Scrunched in the sand, involved in some sort of female game. Tut-tut nose-lifting hair-smoothing lady friends filling tiny plastic plates and

cups and pitchers with sand and snippets of grass and
painstakingly plucked apart pink-and-white clover blossoms.
Inviting each other over for tea or dinner, tasting each other's
cakes and cookies and roast chickens, screwing up their features in approval or distaste

Seldom, only very seldom does Lin force herself to sit at
the edge of the sandbox with them and sip at the sticky little
cups and lick her lips and raise her eyebrows — Ooh, Mrs.
Smith, you put too much *sugar* in it!

Angela's blond curls move closer to Marina's straight
light-brown locks. The two heads are dry now, rinsed of
womb muck and pressed dry with a towel, never again will
my daughters be newborn babies but the dance is perpetually
newborn, the dance does not grow so strangely and unpre-
dictably, the dance does not get old, it uses my body to say
what it has to say but it doesn't age or change, I myself will
die, that doesn't matter but how can I dance if my children
are going to die

Angela's hands cup the distance between her mouth and
Marina's left ear. Secret gossip travels the length of the dark
tunnel between them and the two girls exchange glances of
complicity and indignation.

Lin shivers. She cannot work. She sneaks out of the
house like a robber, flattening her body against walls and
casting furtive glances around corners, then walks alone
toward the pond. Halfway there she breaks into a run.

Last year's lily pads have been chewed away by winter
but their stems remain, still reaching past the water's sur-

face, some straight, others bent at right or wrong angles, still others curling and unfurling, each shape reflected symmetrically by the liquid mirror so that the entire motionless surface seems an ancient stone engraved with some inscrutable alphabet, the runes or hieroglyphs of a vanished people bearing testimony to a vanished world.

Lin stands there, reading the pond.

Thumb in mouth, Marina stares at Lin as she steps into her panties.

And I myself in Bess's bedroom how many decades ago, eyes widening as I watched the heavy hips force themselves into an elastic girdle, the hairy legs nose their way down nylon stockings, the off-white panties flop upward, the great empty-cupped brassiere swing into place, the fingers fumble with hooks and stays behind the fleshy back, and the spilling-over stomach mercifully disappear at last beneath an apricot rayon slip — oh cover it, cover it —

Is that what Marina is thinking now?

Sidney and Violet have taken the girls to the coast for a week.

Lin and Derek make love on the living-room floor. The kitchen table. Standing in the bathroom, arms propped on the sink. They throw a party and their friends come, all of them are young still, despite their disillusionment and their irony, none of them has died of cancer yet, they consume a huge amount of alcohol but Lin drinks nothing at all because she yearns to dance

and then she dances, without a partner, her body thrashing and thrashing all by itself

but this thing will not be gotten rid of, no it will not go, something is terribly terribly wrong, something is impossible

Here, Mommy!

They bring her gifts of flowers and pebbles, shells and straws.

Here Mommy!

tearing off an all-but-invisible bit of weed to hold out to her when they kiss her hello or good-bye

gift gift smile gift —

Here, Mommy, this is for you!

Look, Mommy!
Look, Daddy!

Looking is what confers existence on their daughters' drawings, colorings, mudpies, Lego constructions, choice of clothing, efforts at ballet.

Look, Mommy!

Angela on tiptoes in her brand-new pointes. Teetering, arms in fifth position, toes squashed, crushed. She lifts one leg, stretches her arms out in an awkward arabesque, loses her balance, tries again.

How was that? Not bad for a first try, huh? You think I'll be a better dancer than you are, some day? Did you do as well as that the first time you tried pointes? Huh? Did you?

Oh no, says Lin. The first time I tried pointes, I fell on my face so often my teacher suggested I try wearing one on my nose.

Really? Angela laughs delightedly.

Working on her pointes in the streetlamp-lit living room, long after Joe and Bess had gone to bed, using the edge of the poker table as a barre. Long hours of fouettés, allongés, developpés, ronds de jambe and soubresauts alone in the middle of the night. Her jaws clenched in determination. Ignoring the dull ache in her neck, in the small of her back, especially in her calves. The next morning, she would wash the blood from her toes and hobble off to school.

Mommy, is it nice to be grown-up? asks Angela.
    Lin thinks this over.
Yes it is, she says.
Now bend down and ask me, And is it nice to be little?
    Lin bends down.
And is it nice to be little?
Yes it is.

The children are in bed upstairs, Lin can feel their dreams above her, two layers luminous and light in the cricket-streaked silence. Derek is reading his students' papers, leaning forward over his desk in the corner, smoking his pipe.
    Lin stares at his back.

No matter what I do, Rachel tells Lin over the telephone, Sean says I love Plato more than him. I *love* him, God knows — but it's all getting so frighteningly dark . . . We're starting to make hatred with our bodies instead of love, Lin, I'm afraid we'll end up fucking ourselves to death.

Why don't you come over for dinner tonight? says Lin.

Once the children have been tucked in and kissed good-night, Derek serves highballs for the three of them next to the fireplace. Rachel is already tipsy, her speech perceptibly slurred — she didn't use to drink this much, thinks Lin — and she can talk of nothing but Sean.

The problem, she says, is that we've both been hooked on hopelessness since we were kids. Child addicts, as it were. Not only that, but we're both used to having the monopoly on misery. So now we fight about who gets to be more miserable.

Sounds to me like a healthy basis for a relationship, says Derek.

We're both past masters of the withering gaze, Rachel continues, and we simply can't turn it off. So now he's started training his on Plato and Kant and Feuerbach — and all my elaborate systems of defense are burning to a crisp.

And what do you train yours on? inquires Derek.

On his poetry, naturally. I tell him, Sean, you know, you're just the opposite of Walt Whitman, you spend your time enumerating all the things you despise.

And Sean? Asks Lin.

And Sean says Baby, that's because my *Song of Myself* has always been one long, reverberating silence.

Derek pours the three of them another drink.

The other day, Rachel goes on, we went for a walk in the cemetery and he asked me to look into the price of a concession. That way, he said, when our friends ask how we're ever going to swing it together, a philosophy professor and a poet, we can tell them Well, it's true a few details do still need ironing out — *but we've got the plots!*

Gee, this guy is delightful, says Derek.

What do *you* think makes him so morbid? asks Lin.

Three guesses, says Rachel.

His mother, his mother, his mother, says Lin.

Ten out of ten, says Rachel.

He hates his mother? asks Derek.

Oh, no, says Rachel. He worships her. Ah, if only he'd been able to hate her — for giving him a series of drunken violent stepfathers, for cowering under their blows year after year, for wielding her impotence over him like a cudgel — he might just have made it.

Made what, though? says Derek.

Yeah, that's always the problem, isn't it? says Rachel.

Well, made something other than poetry, right.

Angela in bed with them.

This is the sound of the wind blowing, she says — whoo-oo, whoo-oo — and this is the sound of time passing —

She falls silent.

Don't talk with your mouth full, Derek tells Marina.

Marina spits a large, half-masticated piece of sausage onto her plate and goes on talking.

Opening night in New York. Emile is with her in her hotel room; they are watching the evening news. As always Lin is wracked with pain but she knows that in just a few hours her thoughts will be sucked down the black funnel into that other world and she will manage, more than manage, triumph. The stone, the sculpture, the failure and madness, the imprisonment — flesh tingles with the anticipation of this duo. And it could change the course of her career; there is talk of Europe . . .

Then the phone rings. Emile answers it, covers the receiver with his hand.

It's Derek, he says. Should I tell him to call back in the morning?

No, no, says Lin. If he's calling on opening night it must be important. I'll take it.

But when he presses the receiver to her ear, Angela is on the line.

Mommy? Mommy, you know what, I have pink taste.

You do, do you?

Yup. It's serious to have pink taste, you know.

Why's that?

Because you cry every time.

Every time what?

Every time you hear a sad story.

Oh, baby . . .

Then Marina. Why on earth has Derek allowed the girls to do this, call her — Marina's tiny angry voice, whining, pleading, saying Mommy? Mommy, where are you? — as if

Lin had played a trick on her by shrinking and hiding herself
in the receiver — Mommy, come home! please Mommy,
please Mommy, please come home! Mommy I want you!
Mommy!

Lin slams down the receiver. She will murder Derek
when she gets home.

There must be space inside her body, vast expanses of
empty space, for her to be able to confront the space outside,
the universe
    and now there is that voice, like a hand
    tugging at her voluminous velvet skirt
    trying to prevent her from walking up the four steps to
the stage
    she concentrates on the audience — the human beings
who have entered this hall and are now fidgeting and sniffing
in their seats, brains abuzz with worries and memorized telephone numbers and jetsam of this evening's news
    it is Lin's responsibility to obliterate all of this
    yes, pare it away, clean to the still white bone
    she knows, she knows how to do it — first you satisfy
them, and then you do far more than satisfy them, you carry
them with you, beyond what they were hoping, yearning for,
farther and farther into astounding effort, amazing grace —
    The applause crashes like breakers. She bathes in it,
washes the sweat from her skin in it, soothes her burning
brow in it
    but she knows the dance was damaged

Marina is ill with leprosy. Her skin is rotting, peeling off her face, her hands, her feet. Her body is wasting away, she is dying, Lin can see her heart beating more and more feebly through her chest like a starving mouse trapped in its cage of ribs.

She wakes in her Manhattan hotel room, drenched in sweat and violent sunlight. She looks at the clock — past noon — she had gone to bed at four. Marina's heart — *the conductor's beat for the entire symphony of your pregnancy* — it seems so long ago her doctor said those lovely words . . .

Arms round her knees, Lin huddles shivering in the sunlight that glances off the sheets. Then she bolts to the bathroom, sweating green drops of bile

but she cannot vomit

and there is her hairdresser's appointment at two

and her concentration to be found, somehow, refound,

before tonight's performance

The season advances imperturbably.

In a single night the leaves are ripped from their branches by a wind crazed as a rapist.

November bows out with a flourish and December rolls in like a bass drum. Lin has said no to Europe, without even mentioning the invitation to Derek. There is something too grim going on inside of her.

One clear bitter-cold afternoon the doorbell rings and she hurtles down the two flights of stairs, disheveled and pre-occupied. It is Rachel looking like a crow, her features pinched out of shape by the cold, nose and chin sharpened, black hair swept rakish. Lin takes her friend in her arms, aghast at how she is trembling, and how thin she feels through the heavy coat.

I will love that man until I die, says Rachel, and her voice is gray ash.

Lin makes them tea.

Rachel, she says. Sean Farrell is not worthy of painting your pretty toenails.

He's the only person who ever made me want to live. And he promised me he'd want to live, too, if only I'd live with him. But as soon as I moved in he broke his promise — he still prefers to die! Every day I come home from work and find him sitting there on the edge of the bed, hunched over his gin and tonic like a dog over its bone — and he *snarls* at me.

Sean is a sick man, says Lin. He can't live with anybody, let alone a serious beautiful lady like you.

But he's so helpless! And so funny . . . Once I asked him, very timidly, what he felt like if he went for twenty-four hours without a drink, if it made him ill or nasty or anything, and he gave me the sweetest little twisted smile and he said To tell you the truth, my dear Rachel, *I don't know.*

Gee, I don't think that's funny at all, says Lin. I also think you're getting hideously thin.

Rachel closes her eyes to flush back tears. Then, opening them, she grins with self-irony.

Why is it, she says, that I still feel as if I didn't have the right to get up in the morning? Huh Lin, can you tell me that? As if I had to sort of sneak into the day, you know? Slink into existence, hoping that no one will notice the imposture.

And that the sun will consent to shine on you along with everyone else? says Lin, remembering this image from their teenage years.

Exactly, says Rachel. It wouldn't dare make a dark spot just for me, would it? The whole world is flooded with light and here I am being followed around by a spot-dark!

The two of them laugh together, but Lin is worried about her friend.

Derek grasps the tight warm ball of Marina's crouched body beneath the armpits and swings her up into the air.
What*ever* you do, he says on the first swing
I *don't* want you, he says on the second, higher swing to *touch* the ceiling! — on the third and highest swing Marina stretches out her chubby legs, kicks the ceiling and yells with laughter at Derek's feigned astonishment. Again! Do it again! she squeals

She loves this game.
What*ever* you do — I *don't* want you — to *touch* the ceiling!

Lin is listening to them from behind her newspaper.

One winter's day Nijinsky took his little girl Kyra out for a walk. They were standing at the edge of a frozen pond and laughing at the skaters slipping and falling on the ice when a man came up to them. *Aren't you Nijinsky?* he asked. The dancer nodded. *Will your charming daughter follow in your footsteps? Oh, no!* said Nijinsky. *Her grandfather only knew how to walk, her father only knows how to dance, but she — she must fly!* And so saying, he picked Kyra up and tossed her into the air. *You shall fly, shan't you, Kyra?* he shouted gaily, and the little girl squealed with delight. Nijinsky went on tossing her into the air, higher and higher, dangerously high it seemed to the onlooker — but the little girl's peals of laughter kept ringing out, she was utterly confident in the hands of her father, the love of her father — yes she would fly, she was already flying —

What*ever* you do — I *don't* want you — to *touch* the ceiling!

Derek throws Marina into the air but this time she

escapes his grasp, her feet go through the roof and her body speeds skyward, tumbling madly amidst the clouds, head over heels until it is out of sight —

Lin slams her newspaper down on her lap. This has to stop. Something has got to stop.

They are standing on the bridge. There is snow on either bank but the river isn't frozen over yet. Marina is dropping sticks and stones into the water. The pebbled path leading to the bridge is a spilled treasure chest. How does she know which stones to choose?

Why do all children love throwing stones into the water? Lin asks Derek.

What do you mean, why? It's wonderful, isn't it?

Lin thinks about it. She no longer knows what is wonderful and what is not. She is very, very tired. Please don't climb up on the bridge, Marina, you're scaring me.

Are you afraid I'm gonna drown?

Yes.

Marina's thumb-sucking, now that she is two and a half, is no longer endearing, it is disquieting. She sucks her thumb until the skin is raw, they baste it with Mercurochrome but she licks the Mercurochrome off, and when scabs form she eats the scabs. She speaks around her thumb. Her sentences are gummy and garbled.

How long do you think Marina will go on sucking her thumb? asks Lin.

Let her suck her thumb, says Derek. I sucked mine until I was ten and look what a nice person I turned out to be.

But she sucks it so hard — as if she were starving!

Don't worry about it, says Derek.

We are the mothers of the hungry dead . . . chanted the dancers of Graham's *Deep Song. We are the mothers of the hungry living* . . . The only hope I have of surmounting this fear is to face it, embrace it, dance it. Dance the dance of mothers whose children are dying because they are living, the dance of mothers whose children are dead.

Sidney and Violet are between leisure resorts, visiting.
Derek is in the kitchen, making them Sunday roast beef and
green beans and mashed potatoes with gravy. So what are you
working on these days, Lin? Says Violet, plumping herself
down on the leather couch so heavily that it wheezes.

A piece called *Pietà,* says Lin.

I never did understand what makes you young women of
today so ambitious.

She lowers her voice to a hoarse whisper.

I was never in love with Sidney, he took me away from my
mother, that was the only reason I married him — but if I'd
been lucky enough to have a husband like yours — for which
I take no credit, don't get me wrong, I'm not boasting about
my son — but a brilliant man who writes books about philosophy and earns a full professor's salary into the bargain —
believe me, I'd never have dreamed of working!

She had not dreamed of it anyway, whereas her husband
had been the harassed and ulcer-prone owner of a dress fac-
tory in the Bronx.

Do you really think a man with a mind like Derek's should be
wasting so much of his time in the kitchen? Violet insists.

Oh, but he makes excellent roast beef, says Lin.

Violet glances sharply at her daughter-in-law but cannot
determine whether this was meant to be ironic. So what's this
Pietà about? she asks. Isn't that some sort of Virgin Mary
sculpture?

One of my dancers will be playing the Virgin Mary, Lin nods

reluctantly. Another plays Hecuba, another Niobe, and so forth . . .

Derek calls them to the table.

Oh! groans Violet with visible relief, heaving herself to her feet. I don't know what's the matter with me, I'm famished! My stomach is growling as if it hadn't seen food in a week.

Well, it has been a full two and a half hours since your last croissant, murmurs Sidney, setting aside the real-estate section of the *Times*.

Shut up, Sidney. Don't try to be funny, it never works.

The girls gobble down their meal and vanish.

They sure are terrific little kids, says Violet. You must be proud of them, Lin.

No, says Lin.

Pardon me?

No, I'm not. It's dangerous to be proud of your children. Don't you know the story of Niobe?

Derek looks at her warningly.

If it's not in the Old Testament or on TV, says Sidney, my wife doesn't know about it.

Niobe was the queen of Thebes, says Lin. She had so many beautiful sons and daughters and she was so proud of them that she defied Leto, the goddess of fertility, and Leto punished her by killing each and every one of her children.

Could I have a little more gravy please? says Sidney.

A German dancer named Mary Wigman, Lin pursues doggedly, performed a *Dance of Niobe* for the women of Berlin in 1942.

For the women of Berlin in 1942, Violet repeats, her voice a knife blade.

Yes. She said that though the dance lasted only a few minutes, at the end of each performance she felt as if she had aged by many years.

Isn't that a shame, says Violet, setting down her fork ostentatiously to let them know her appetite has been spoiled.

Lin is washing the pots and pans. In 1942 Mary Wigman was fifty-six years old; it was too late for her to bear a child but not too late to dance, and so she danced for the women of Berlin. Hands pressed to stomach, a lullabye wafting sweetly from her lips, she tried to protect the life inside of her — but then her eyes dilated with fear her throat choked back a cry her body dropped to the ground as if struck by lightning her arms strove to hug this last child to herself — Take me! take me, she said but spare this little one, spare my last child — and at the end there was nothing left, nothing but her empty body, a charred and empty jar. In Lin's new work, the *Pietàs* — twenty women dressed in long white flowing gowns — or red, yes, red perhaps — will form a chain and slowly pass the corpses of their sons from hand to hand — the male dancers limp, inert, their limbs heavy-slack — and the chain of women will undulate and they will chant and sway, intense deep chords, slow inexorable rhythms, conveying this endless mourning of mothers for their murdered sons, perhaps the only unity the human race will every manage to achieve —

Derek returns from accompanying his parents to the car. When he speaks to her is voice is low, and this is a bad sign. You can't just say anything, Lin, on the pretext that it's true.

Lin wheels on him.

For Christ's sake can't you *see?* she cries. Leto was superior to Niobe not because she was a goddess but because *her children couldn't die!*

You scare me sometimes, murmurs Derek after a pause, shaking his head and lighting his pipe.

All his life, thinks Lin, he'll go on shaking his head and lighting his pipe when he's at loss for words.

Her outburst has brought Angela to the kitchen. She stands there uncertainly in the doorway, eyes wide, and Lin abruptly turns her back.

What's the matter with Mommy, Daddy?

Their lovemaking is abominable that night. Derek pins Lin's knees against her chest and simply pounds into her, she cannot move, when she struggles to get out from under him he turns her over, crushes her face into the pillow and goes on pounding, she cannot breathe, she wants to spoil his pleasure, how dare he — her body is not made for this, it is made for enchantment —

her body can be anything
immutable inscrutable stone
or a feather, a mote, a sunspot —

Sometimes when we make love, he says to her afterward —

and his tone makes it one of the nastiest things he has ever said — I have the feeling you're choreographing me.

Lin and Derek are driving home, they have left the girls in the house alone, why did we leave them all by themselves, why, something will have happened to them, how can we possibly have gone out without them . . . As they approach the house they see the swing in the backyard swinging all by itself, up and down, very high, as if propelled by a pair of invisible legs . . . Hurry, says Lin, wild with anguish — park the car! Then she is running, tearing open the gate

but the front door is guarded by six or seven dogs, huge beasts unrestrained by any leash, barking and slavering with fury

Lin gets down on her haunches and barks at them in turn

rasping, howling, her voice rips through her vocal chords and leaves her throat raw

A dog leaps at her and she — she, Lin, who has always been afraid of dogs — rises to break its leap in midair with her arm. Then she slips both hands into its mouth and braces her fingers against its sharp teeth and yanks at its jaws until the jawbones snap

yes she breaks its very head apart with her bare hands

Mommy, says Angela, Marina is killing Lula.

Lula is Marina's favorite doll, she is sprawled naked on her back on the kitchen table and Marina is stabbing her cloth stomach with forks and knives. She looks up when Lin walks in.

She's sick, she explains matter-of-factly. I have to give her some shots or she's gonna die.

Over the telephone Rachel's voice is small and tense and bad.

Can you get in your car and drive over here right away asks Lin.

I don't think so.

You took some stuff?

Yes.

Goddammit, Rachel.

Outside it is a snowing and blowing, already darkening afternoon. Lin zips and buttons the children's coats, ties and tucks their scarves, holds boots for Marina — Push, darling, push hard now, that's right — wriggles their hands into gloves — Okay now spread your fingers apart, each finger has to go into its own house, okay? Hey, what's number Three doing in number Four's house? Is this visiting day or something?

Finally they are in Rachel's driveway.

Stay in the car, I'll be right back.

The front door is unlocked. Rachel's bedroom is not a pretty sight, or a pretty smell.

What day is it? asks Rachel.

Lin half walks, half carries her friend to the bathroom, sits her on the toilet lid and turns the bath taps on full blast. She makes a ball of Rachel's soiled bedding and stuffs it into the closet.

In the car, Angela and Marina are giggling hysterically.

Mommy, Mommy, Marina wet her pants!

I couldn't help it, says Marina.

She was laughing too hard, explains Angela, and you told us to stay in the car.

Come on in the house for a while, we'll change your pants
later.

Rachel has peeled off her clothes and climbed into the
tub. Lin sponges her knobby back and combs her tangled
hair, humming under her breath.

By the time they leave, night has fallen and the wind is
chasing clouds across a full moon. Looking up the sky,
Marina says,
Why is the moon all torn apart, Mommy?

Was it Sean? asks Derek, propped on his right elbow in bed,
his left hand resting between Lin's thighs.
I don't think so, says Lin. She just wants to die, that's all.
Her students worship her, says Derek.

His hand is moving now and Lin does not answer. She
can feel his member stiff and motionless at her side as his fingers strum her, filling her body with the tense music of
Spanish guitar, the stamping feet and tossed heads of fla-
menco dancers, the bright red lipstick of the woman's defiant
smile, black lace mantilla mixed with her black hair, black
lace floating like froth above the full cream curves of her
breasts, the man's tight pants and sarcastic glance bespeaking
murder, Carmen, murder, flashing daggers and flashing eyes,
lips parted in silent screams, the guitar playing louder and
faster now, its chords angry and clashing, and the tension in
her loins is that of the toreador arched to stab the bull, and at
last the taut skin is pierced, it bursts and the red blood flows,

she is coming and coming and, opening her eyes, she floods her pleasure into Derek's eyes which are on her face.

The waves die down. She curls her fingers round her husband's rigid cock and plummets into slumber.

I had a dream, says Angela the next morning at breakfast. I was at school with my friends and it was time for our mothers to come and pick us up, but instead of our mothers a bunch of witches came, they'd eaten all the mothers and all the policemen and now they were coming to get the children. And in the middle of the classroom, there was this giant spider hanging from the ceiling and telling us sad stories.

Lin stares at her, speechless. Derek burst out laughing. The part about eating the policemen is brilliant, he says. Making sure that all possible paths to salvation have been cut off.

Lin visits Rachel in the clinic where she is recovering. She looks both sheepish and serene, as if her brush with death had done her good.

You know, Lin says to her, I sometimes feel that if I look at the kids too closely, they'll disappear. Just melt into nothingness like leprechauns.

It's the other way around, says Rachel. Leprechauns disappear if you take your eyes *off* them.

But I mean, it's scary, says Lin. You wind them up in your womb and they go buzzing around like robots for the rest of their lives, you know? They learn how to talk, they kiss you good-night, they shed their successive clothing sizes like so many skins . . . They don't really need you.

What are you talking about? says Rachel, frowning. Of course they need you.

There is a silence. Then Lin blurts out,

I've been asked to go to Mexico.

So go to Mexico, Rachel sighs, sinking back in her pillow. When do you leave?

To direct a company, I mean. Next year.

Next *year?* You mean *all* next year?

Rachel stares at her.

I don't know what you're talking about, Lin, she says at last. You're supposed to be here to comfort me and instead you try to give me a heart attack.

Forget it, says Lin. Please. Forget it.

Winter break arrives and Derek suggests they spend a week together, the four of them, in New York.

This is certainly a good idea, thinks Lin,

it must be

In the car on the way down, Marina throws cookies out the window. Lin is driving, her stomach roils with blood and her mood is bleak.

How much farther? How much farther? How much farther? ask the girls, so often that within half an hour Derek and Lin are as bored as they are, as bored as when they themselves were children and their parents took them on interminable car trips. Look at the countryside, says Lin, just as Bess used to say to her, to make her shut up.

The countryside is in fact growing rather hideous and Lin is thinking of Mexico, of the Cyd Charisse dances in *Sombrero* — pummeled by rain, water streaming from her hair down her face and neck and back, her living body leaping enthrallingly amidst the monumental still stone bodies of the gods, dancing in a frenzy of beauty and affirmation, her cobalt blue dress soaked through and clinging to the cream of her thighs, her breasts and that smile! Oh the marvelous flashing teeth of Cyd Charisse, her insolent joy as she braved the storm and whirled, climbed, slid and tumbled among the statues, utterly alone and strong . . . Mexico. What it means to have a body in such a place. The flame of the dance defying the impassive eternal shadows of the pyramids. The fugitive challenging the final. Life thumbing its nose at death and winning — winning — yes, before it loses . . .

Angela needs to go pee, says Derek.
I gotta go, I gotta go, says Angela.
There's a rest stop half a mile ahead, says Derek.

In the Manhattan department store, Marina wanders off
and gets sucked up in the whirlwind of Christmas shoppers.
Sweating in her fur coat, arms aching with the weight of
bags, Lin drags Angela up and down aisles and escalators
looking for her . . .
I thought you abandoned me, says Marina in the street. I
thought I was never going to see you again.
But darling, says Lin, head pounding. I'll never ever abandon
you. I'll always be there when you need me.
Except when you're dead.
Yes. Except when I'm dead.
You could kill yourself on purpose just to hurt my feelings,
says Marina.

The day after their return, a Sunday, Derek takes the girls
to the park all morning so that Lin can work in peace. She
plunges deeply into the *Pietà* movements, forgets where and
who she is, allows her body to be invaded by the agony of
maternal grief, stylizes the timeless gestures of tearing out
hair and raking chest with nails, translates the flood gush of
tears into skittering mad-bird hands, translates the raw throat
of keening into geometrical rolls on the floor —
    At last — hearing the front door open and family sounds
spill into the hall — she stops. And is frightened, coming

downstairs, at how far away she had been while she stayed home and the others went out. She kisses Derek, peeling off her sticky leotards.

You're drenched to the bone, he says.

I know, I'll take a shower before lunch, says Lin, stripping to nearly naked as she hobbles across the living room. But Angela wants to kiss her too and then Marina is whining for her turn, and when Lin sinks strengthless to the couch the little girl is suddenly all over her, licking the sweat off her arms, licking and licking her neck, her face, licking the way a she-cat licks her kittens — You're all salty, Mommy, you taste so good! — but it is not quite pleasant, not quite all right, Marina is not quite young enough anymore for this to be sweetly innocent. Lin counts to ten before pushing her gently but firmly from her lap.

The girls are talking animatedly in Marina's room, door ajar, when Lin walks past.

The eyes rot, too, Angela is saying.

What about the muscles? asks Marina.

Of course. Everything rots except the skeleton.

Even the fingernails?

No, not the fingernails. They keep growing in the tomb.

Oh! But then later, when the fingers rot, do the fingernails fall off?

Lin moves away. Her daughters continue their discussion, but she can no longer hear them.

It is their tenth wedding anniversary. Lin sits on the edge of the bathtub and watches Derek as he shaves, trying to lose herself in these familiar movements that have always made her smile, the way the fingertips of his left hand stretch the skin of his cheek and neck and upper lip, the way his chin thrusts forward involuntarily, the way his mouth twists and swerves to keep out of the razor's path

Then she goes to the front porch and picks up the *Times*

Then she sets the *Times* on the breakfast table and presses her forehead against it

At half past nine, when everyone has left, the doorbell rings. Flowers for their anniversary? No. A telegram

it is from Bess

the postman goes sauntering back down the steps

the envelope is open

heart attack she reads, and then

died she reads, and then

Joe she reads, she cannot glue the words together to make a sentence

She stands in the hallway with the telegram in her hand. From the corner of her eye she can see herself in the full-length mirror. She sees that she is beautiful, and that the hand holding the telegram is long and white and curved like the neck of a swan, and that the telegram is the same blue as the silk of her trousers, only paler. The letters tremble on the page. The funeral is to be held the next day.

She takes a taxi to the university and interrupts Derek's

seminar, feeling wide-eyed and pale and poignant in front on the students. In his office she tells him. He folds her to his body.

I can't drive out there, she says. I wouldn't trust myself to drive.

Darling, he says, you don't even have to go if you don't feel like it.

Yes, I do have to go. I'll take the train. Bess can meet me at the station. I'll call her tonight. I'll take the girls with me.

Not both of them, says Derek — take Angela.

No, says Lin. I'll take Marina. She never met my dad. I love you, Derek. Do you know that?

Yes.

Can you stop off and buy a little black dress for Marina on your way home?

Angela is jealous of her sister's new dress.

The next morning, Marina watches Lin as she packs for the trip.

You're the most beautiful mommy in the whole world, she says. You're as beautiful as Italy! But you should choose clothes that go better with your eyes and lips and hair.

Lin says nothing.

You've got stripes on your forehead, Marina goes on.

They're not stripes, says Lin, they're lines. Because I'm starting to get old and ugly.

I wish you'd be old and ugly right away.

Why's that?

So I could make fun of you.

At breakfast Marina drops her glass of orange juice and it smashes to the floor. On the train a paper cup of water leaps from her hand and splashes across the pages of an old man's magazine. At noon, in the greasy spoon where they have lunch with Bess, she overturns a full bowl of hot mushroom soup on the skirt of Lin's black suit. Lin scrubs the skirt in the downstairs bathroom with a moistened paper towel that rapidly disintegrates, leaving white flecks on the black wool which are impossible to remove

whereas her father is dead

Don't worry, Ma'am, says the waitress. We'll have that cleaned up in a jiffy. You can just change tables and we'll bring her another bowl of soup. Sure is a cute little girl you've got there.

I love you, says Marina, staring straight into the waitress's face.

Bess, clearly fuddled with alcohol, calls Marina Angela six times on the way to the cemetery. She has bleached her hair blond and her complexion is unhealthily ruddy beneath her cheap black hat. Lin puts her arm around her stepmother's shoulders and squeezes hard, overcome with pity for this woman who has just lost the single thing that gave a shape to her days. What will become of her?

We'll take care of you Bess, she murmurs. Then she withdraws her arm uncomfortably, knowing that what she means is that they will send her money.

The graveyard is rain and mud and artificial flowers. Lin recognizes a handful of men as her father's garage employees and poker partners of twenty years before . . . The name of the game is High and low! Pregnant threes! One-eyed jacks! How would you gentlemen feel about a seven-card stud with follow-the-lady wild? Come on, ante up, ante up, how many do you want? I'll stay pat, Joe, thanks just the same, quite happy with what I've got. These men who stank of axle grease and beer had never seemed young to Lin, but now she sees they must have been young at the time. Dance this, dance this . . .

As of the very first words of the ceremony Marina starts to whimper, so Lin picks her up and holds her in her arms. There is no way to hold this long unwieldy body and an umbrella at the same time. Rain runs down both their necks, Marina's dangling boots daub the front of Lin's trench coat with mud and the event of her father's death recedes still further into the background.

In the train again, Marina leans forward and says to the elderly lady sitting across from them,

You have a silver tooth.

The lady blushes.

No, it isn't silver, she demurs.

But it isn't white.

No, unfortunately. I'd love to have beautiful white teeth like yours.

I brush mine. Didn't you brush yours?

Across the aisle a couple bursts into laughter and the elderly lady joins in gratefully. But Lin, jerking her daughter back in her seat, whispers poisonously,
I don't want to hear another word out of you for the rest of the trip. Is that clear?

Lin is listening to the radio as she irons

This morning she has interrupted her ironing a dozen times to switch stations, burning a dish towel in her nervous goings back and forth

but the music will not come where the fear is

She lifts a pair of Derek's pants from the basket

sets them on the ironing board as though they were heavy

looks at them

First she will iron the legs without worrying about the creases. Yes, this is all right. Then she tries to fold the pants to get the crease straight on both sides. She starts ironing from the bottom, but by the time she reaches the thigh the cloth is crumpled underneath. She watches her hands smooth the dark linen flat and pick up the iron and press bad wrinkles into the material. Her movements speed up uncontrollably, she turns the pants over and over, what she is doing no longer has anything to do with ironing. Finally she sits down and squeezes her hands beneath her armpits to force them to stop moving.

Where's my Lula? demands Marina.

Maybe you left her in the bathroom, says Lin.

As Marina opens the bathroom door to check, Derek spots her doll lying under the kitchen table.

Hey, Marina, he says. Lula's right here!

No, says Marina. I left her in the bathroom.

But I have her right here in my hand, sweetheart, says Derek.

Marina comes out of the bathroom livid with rage, strides over to her father and brandishes an empty hand in his face. Lula's right here! she screams. I told you I left her in the bathroom.

Then she grabs the doll from Derek and runs away.

It is again, yet again a Sunday morning and the girls have prepared a puppet show for their parents. Lin is not allowed to drink her coffee first, she must watch The Seven Little Goats.

Marina is the wolf. When he decides to dip his paw into flour to fool the kids into thinking he is their mother, Angela pours the entire contents of the flour canister onto her sister's sock-puppet wolf . . . and all over the living-room rug.

Lin bursts into tears.

Derek vacuums the rug, shaking his head.

Marina turns four and Lin organizes a party. She goes through the motions, sets up the games, always the same games, but no fun can be injected into them. The afternoon drags and grinds, fights break out over toys and Lin is rapidly overwhelmed. What is it I dread? she wonders. That the noise will just keep on getting louder and the children more rambunctious until the whole house explodes?

The mothers arrive punctually at six to pick up their off-spring, parking their cars in a neat line in the driveway. Lin does not want to speak to them.

Then the house is empty at last.

Marina walks into the kitchen where Lin is tidying up.
Mommy, she snivels, there's hardly any balloons left!
What do you mean, hardly any? There are four balloons right here on the floor.
No, there isn't! Look! One, two, *two*, TWO!

Lin leaps across the kitchen and slaps Marina's face as hard as she can.

She is sitting on the bed, stroking the bedspread. Derek is tying his tie. They are invited out for dinner, the baby-sitter will be here in a few minutes and Lin has not yet finished getting dressed. She is wearing stockings and a slip. She strokes the bedspread with her right hand. Why should it take so long to get it smooth, utterly smooth?

Lin?

She starts.

It's quarter of.

Derek leaves the room. Lin rises, pulls a dress over her head, slips her feet into some shoes. She is ready. She hears the children's high-pitched voices greeting their baby-sitter, the young woman responding warmly, Derek saying something funny.

It is over. She is ready.

That night in bed she listens intently to the hiss of the radiator in their room. Hour after hour, she strains to understand.

Part Two

THE COMPANY

The time was ripe. It had ripened in the cold white heart of winter and fallen to the ground.

Lin is dancing in Mexico City. Her feet are bare and her body is enormous, bigger then ever before. She is Cihuacoatl, the awesome Aztec goddess of war and childbirth. She knows everything, can do anything, will stop at nothing.

She is working with clumsiness. She makes her dancers fall and fall, recalling the way Joe's poker friends would sometimes tumble from their chairs at dawn and crash to the floor without even waking up. And the way small children fall — again and again, almost methodically — running up or down the stairs, riding their bikes, dashing down side-walks, so confident of where they're headed, so exhilarated they seem to be airborne, and when — trip, splat — the hard flat concrete slams into their chests, always they look up with the same expression of stunned surprise on their faces, before the tears.

It's falling, not leaping, that makes the dream of weightless-ness come true, says Lin. Accept the floor, cherish the floor — all the upward energy comes from downward.

She loves the woosh of the group, melded by her mind into a single being — enthused heated radiant, creating leap-ing electric unison — and her dancers worship her. Never have they had so much sheer fun in rehearsals, or worked so hard. They would be prepared, she feels, to break every bone in their bodies for her.

Yes it is for this that I was born
and nothing — no, *nothing* —
can equal this joy of making bodies move through space
filling the air with movement

responding to music with silences in scansion
leaps and bounds
the soundless cries of all the pain and pleasure in the
universe

In her dream her mother appears to her. Marilyn, Lin
whispers when she sees her, astounded at how very young she
is, much younger than herself, still barely twenty years old.
Marilyn gazes at her daughter in silence for a long while.
There is overwhelming compassion in her eyes. So you too
have become a runaway, she says at last, softly and sadly. But
no, Mother, Lin protests. You don't understand. It may look
the same from the outside but it's not at all the same thing,
not at all — let me explain . . . At this point Marilyn's eyes
overflow with tears and the tears cause her face to dissolve,
first into watery planes of color, then into blankness.

Mommy had to go away, says Derek. She's gone on a long long trip, we won't be seeing her again for quite a while. You mean she's dead? says Marina.

Derek spends the first night sitting up in his bed which is no longer their bed, eyes closed but unsleeping, allowing what has just become his reality to permeate him.

I need to dance . . .

He is surprised at his own lack of surprise

and realizes he has known this for a long time, perhaps from the beginning.

When a week has gone by, he calls Theresa.

Mrs. Lhomond is out of town, he tells her lamely. I was wondering if you might be able to come in again, a few hours a week.

He knows that upon arriving the next day, Theresa will understand as soon as she sets her eyes on his face, and that she will ask no questions but remove her shoes, put on her slippers and calmly take the vacuum cleaner from the closet in which she put it away several years ago.

He finds this image oddly reassuring; that night he falls asleep more easily than usual.

Alone in her bedroom, Marina is sucking her thumb. The cars that pass in front of the house at intervals cast moving squares of light on the walls near her bed. She has to smack her hand onto one of the luminous spots — quick,

quick — if she wants to avoid having a bad dream.

Sometimes this method works, and sometimes it does not.

Tonight, she fails to touch the light every single time. It's as if the cars sneaked up on her, dazzled her and then vanished. If she stands at the window to watch for them, she won't have time to run over and touch the walls. She does not know what to do.

Beneath her tongue's rough caress, her left thumb is covered with soft wrinkles, like her toes, when she lingers too long in the bathtub. Suddenly she bites it, trying to surprise herself, but the resulting pain is disappointing.

Getting out of bed, Marina drags her little chair over to the window and climbs onto it. She shoves the window upward, slips her left thumb into the gap, slams the window down with her right hand

and waits a few seconds, teeth clenched, breathing fiercely through her nose, before reopening the window to release herself

that night no bad dreams are visited upon her

and the next morning she hides her swollen black-nailed thumb under the table

Every day after school, Angela does her demi-pliés, her grand-pliés and her arabesques in Lin's dance room. She breathes in her mother's presence, feels Lin's eyes on her body, hears her voice. Lower your shoulders, good, now spread your toes a little more to have a solid base to stand on, that's right darling, turn your knees well out — yes, exactly!

That's beautiful! What exquisite grace in the curve of your arm! Yes my love, don't worry, I'm with you always, always, I am you

After a few weeks they receive a letter from Lin — and, in the same envelope, the papers Derek must sign for the pronouncement of a Mexican divorce.

When he reads the letter to the girls after supper, there is a note of forced gaiety in this voice.

The city I live in, says the letter, *is the biggest dirtiest city in the whole wide world. It's so polluted that in children's drawings the sky is colored gray instead if blue! But I love it anyway — Someday if it's all right with Daddy you can come and visit me here.*

Is it all right with you, Daddy? asks Angela immediately.

Of course, says Derek. What a silly question.

He notices that Marina's jaws are clenched; she is grinding her teeth.

Later, just after they have gone to bed, he walks past Marina's room and overhears her scolding her Lula doll in a low voice.

If you don't stop whining, she said, I'll go away and never ever *ever* come back!

Derek freezes. He turns around, walks slowly back to his study and signs the divorce papers.

Mommy, *Mommy!* MOMMY!

Derek runs stark naked to Marina's room. Her eyes are glazed, she does not see him, she is seeing inwardly, the dream is continuing and she is screaming, screaming, screaming and he does not know what to do. Her body is frozen in a half-curled position, her straight brown bangs are sticking to her forehead, her pajamas are wet with sweat and she is screaming her soul out.

Derek picks up his tight little frozen sweating daughter and carries her downstairs. She struggles.

I want my Mommy! She screams but she is not saying it to him, she is still in the dream, he sets her on the kitchen counter and presses a damp washcloth to her forehead; this is the worst moment of his life, she is still beside herself with fear and he is still naked, standing there in the kitchen next to his screaming little girl.

The March night is clear with a sickle moon. He picks Marina up again and moves with her to the back porch.

Look at the stars sweetheart, he says in a low voice. Look at the moon. *Look,* Marina!

At last Marina's gaze follows her father's pointed finger, losing itself in the spray of shimmering white powder on black, then focusing on the small sharp C of a moon. There is a long silence.

How many stars are up there, Daddy?

I don't know. Millions and millions. Some of them are so far away we can't even see them.

Just like Mommy, right?

Yeah . . . Mommy's a star, too, you're right.

The child is already drowsing against his shoulder. A faint draft from under the door raises the hair on his testicles.

I'll never make love again, he thinks.

Lin and her company are in Veracruz, working on a new piece. Watching her dancers move, Lin makes frantic notes and sketches on a pad. Words sprout out at angles from other words and arch like fountains — dart — turn — dart — knee crawl — lunge — small rond de jambe — knee vibrations — treading — bourrée — strut — stork — wide low arabesque turn . . . Arrows trace the sweep of arm and leg. She describes, demonstrates, puts on the music, watches, nods and cringes, demonstrates again. She takes the dancers' limbs in her hands and turns them into doves, Indians, oxen, planets, rickety persnickety machines.

They have been given an entire gymnasium for their rehearsals, a wonderful space
    but to get to there every afternoon, they must walk through a playground
    a playground with children playing in it
    little Spanish-speaking boys and girls
    their mothers or nannies, dark haired and heavy thighed, sit knitting and muttering near them on the benches
Isn't there another entrance to the gymnasium? Lin asks the man who has found this space for her. But the answer is no. There is not.
    In the Mexico City subway, and in the streets — everywhere but in the dance — Lin is vulnerable to attack by babies. The second she hears a baby crying panic seizes her. She changes cars, crosses streets — runs, sometimes, to escape the accusatory wails.

At night, though, she does not lie awake aching, wondering what her little girls are doing, what they are thinking about, what they are eating, how they are dressed, what they are learning at school . . . All this is banished from her consciousness by sleeping pills.

For Derek, the worst thing is his body. He cannot bear to contemplate his own flesh.

When he picks up the girls at school, they whoosh across the room or down the hall or down the steps toward him, faces ablaze with joy, shouting Daddy Daddy Daddy, then throwing themselves hard into his arms to be swung off their feet and pressed against his chest.

These are the only moments at which Derek feels his body.

Months go by in the big old house. He finally manages to climb the stairs to the third floor and confront the room from which Angela draws her daily sustenance, Lin's dance room.

All is still and warm, dust sparkles in a ray of sunlight.

The two of them bending over the architect's drawings on the kitchen table, discussing insulation and electricity and angles of light, toting up the bills, their tongues in each other's mouths. He can still taste that red muscle

still smell the smell of her sweat

still hear the high wild cry that sometimes leaped from her like a song when she came, caught in her throat then trickled down and down into deep hot bubbling laughter

and other times, tears

Somehow he had expected to find the mirrors empty. But no — no matter where he looks, his own suffering face stares back at him.

Lin may not have this room anymore, he says to himself, jaws clenched. It will not stand still, waiting for her to return.

When Rachel drops by the following afternoon, plastic has been laid down on the floor, Derek is on a stepladder and the girls are down below. Dressed in smocks, paint speckling their hair and faces and bare feet, they are covering the mirrors with acrylics. When they have finished, all that is left of the mirrors are silver slivers flashing from within a tangled jungle of paint.

Where will Angela practice her ballet? asks Rachel.

I've set up a barre for her in her bedroom, Derek explains.

Later they uncork a bottle of champagne. Rachel sees that Derek's eyes are red; and when their glasses clink she cannot quite meet his gaze.

Marina slips out of bed in the middle of the night, her throat is dry, Daddy told me not to wake him up

But as she enters the kitchen on tiptoe for a glass of water she is brought up short

Derek is there

her father whom she has never seen inactive is sitting at the kitchen table

not sleeping, not reading, just there, head in hands

Silently, Marina turns and goes back up to bed.

Angela had the mumps. She is running a fever, her cheeks are deep red and her eyes are glassy. Derek rings Theresa. Yes, she can stay with her during the day.

As he explains Angela's medications to the cleaning lady,

his stomach is knotted. Angela forgive us, he thinks. Forgive your mother and myself.

Mommy! *Mommy!* MOMMY!

Angela. Five in the morning. Her forehead burns his hand. He gives her her medicine, brings her cool water to drink and strokes her swollen throat. He falls asleep sitting on the floor with his head on her bed, and dreams, as he does nearly every night, of fire. Houses burning, entire neighborhoods in flames. Charred motionless children with black smudges on their faces. Live children sitting next to dead mothers, nuzzling their breasts, stroking their cheeks.

Summer arrives, a summer of abominable heat; Sidney and Violet take the two girls to Florida for two weeks. Angela throws herself into the vigorous arms of the breakers, rides the waves with ecstatic abandon. But Marina has a loathing for the water — when water separates, its droplets slither and slide, flow into one another. Sand is better, whose every grain is sharply distinct from every other grain. She spends her afternoons at the beach counting the grains of sand on her knees.

Weighed down by the heat and solitude, Derek drives into town every day and takes refuge in the library. He misses his students. He misses his daughters. Unable to focus, his thoughts keep veering away from the page in front of him and sliding into the infernal downward spiral of Lin — it has been seven months since she left and suddenly she is there again each morning as he climbs the staircase to the library, spinning amongst the pseudo-Greek marble columns like the ghost of Isadora Duncan, always at the farthest edge of his vision, on the verge of disappearing, and when he pivots violently to grasp the floating hem of her white tunic with his eyes, nothing remains of her but a tremor in the sweltering air.

Derek calls Rachel and asks her out
She has had her black hair cut short
They do not hold hands during the movie
Then her car follows his back to his house
In the kitchen they drink ice-cold beer from the refrigerator without speaking. The day's heat hangs in the air, clogs up their throats. Then at the same instant they look at each other, rise very slowly, embrace. Derek is moved by the fragility of Rachel's body, the way her heart flutters against him like a panicked bird. He draws back, lays his hands on her sharp shoulders.

They shower together, soaping each other in the cool rush of the water.

They lie side by side on Lin and Derek's clean white sheets. A night wind fans them faintly through the window screen.

He reaches out and strokes the short black curve of hair behind her ear.

Each night until the end of August, each of the ten remaining nights until the girls return from Florida, Rachel sleeps with Derek. Sometimes, before they fall asleep, she curls her hand around his limp penis. Sometimes he strokes her bony back and tiny breasts. Sometimes, waking at dawn, he gazes at her motionless light-brown body, lying next to his on the bed.

They are loving Lin, both of them, in this sexlessness.

Then the girls return, sunburnt and blister-lipped and brimming with radio songs, and Rachel vanishes.

Watch out for that Marina, says Violet. She's going to be a tough one, mark my words. Isn't that right, Sidney?
Yes, Violet.
You name it, she did it. Right, Sidney?
Yes, Violet.
She's so obstreperous! Plus she was cheeky and rude to everyone — she even talked back to me. You're not my mother so I don't have to obey you, she told me once — didn't she, Sidney? Have you thought of getting a therapist for her, Derek?

Daddy, says Angela. Are we ever gonna see Mommy again?
I think so, honey. But I don't know just when.
Do you get to talk to her sometimes?
Nope.
I talk to her, you know. In my head.
And does she answer you?
Oh, yes!
What do you talk about?

Well, like I ask her why she went away and she says it's because Marina was so bad she couldn't stand it anymore.

That's not true at all, Angela.

Yes, but in my head that's what she says.

Don't you ever repeat that to Marina. Promise?

I promise.

Lin and her company are in Paris; the newspapers churn with advance praise.

We'll teach this city a lesson. Paris is froth, so we shall all be glasses of champagne. A spoof on the Folies Bergères. Upside-down cancan dancers. Can openers. Cartwheels with missing spokes. Scissor-kicking legs turn into corkscrews, bottles explode, corks go flying, liquid spews, champagne spills all over the floor. The movements swell and swirl, then dissolve into bubbles that pop and vanish. The audience is openmouthed, pindrop silent. The dancers seem to have vanished into thin air. No — the air is moving still, flimsy gossamer waves and glints like the rainbow shimmer at the edge of a dream. Then blackout.

Walking down the Boulevard Saint-Germain, Lin hears behind her — soaring loud and clear in English from the surrounding jumble of French —
Mommy!

It is Angela — Angela's voice — Lin spins around. Her body responds to the voice before her brain, she cannot help it, my daughter, my daughter — she spins around.

A chubby American towhead is tugging at her mother's arm.
Mommy! Mommy! she says, pointing at something in a window display.

Not Angela. Lin's heart rebounds against her ribs like a rubber ball; her stomach heaves; she must lean against a tree as, babbling obliviously, the American tourists go past.

Derek has gotten used to guiding little feet down the legs
of woolen tights

    combine out tangled light-brown hair without provoking
screams

      scraping milk-softened corn flakes into garbage cans

He cuts his daughters' fingernails, their toenails and their
bangs, makes sure they change their socks and underpants,
learns to sew on buttons. He cooks for them, real meals, and
asks them questions about their day at school. Their family
must be a triangle, not a mutilated square. We are holding
hands. We are all here. There is no one missing anywhere.

He sees Rachel nearly every day at the university.
Sometimes in the faculty coffee room they stand staring out
the window at the rain, then the snow, side by side. Neither
of them ever alludes to their August nights.

Marina shreds her sister's schoolbooks, steals her Barbie
dolls. One day in December, out of the blue, she gives Angela
a violent shove from the top of the staircase. There is a blood-
curdling scream and Derek, rushing to the hallway from the
kitchen, finds Angela unconscious at the bottom of the steps.

The air above his head is thick with moving shadows.

How can he possibly punish this little girl?

There must be Christmas, he decides.

He buys a fir tree for the first time in his life and teaches
the girls to count backward — only nineteen days till

Christmas, eighteen, seventeen — but has no idea with what to fill the zero. He lies awake at night, worrying about it. Finally he spends a morning walking up one side of Main Street and down the other, emptying his wallet, filling his briefcase and pockets with trinkets and fluff.

He dumps it all on his desk at the university and stands there much of his lunch hour, staring at the high-heeled Barbie shoes and the kangaroo-spocked socks. The gifts just sit there. Finally they begin to glimmer, and he knows he must be crying again.

On Christmas Eve he hangs his daughters' stockings from the mantelpiece and drinks half a bottle of whiskey.

Marina wakens Angela at seven; together they burst into his room and drag him from his dreams. Derek senses something hideous in their eagerness. They are like hunting dogs, yapping after a fox they long to tear limb from limb.
Go see what's in your stocking while I make myself a cup of coffee, he tells them, head throbbing.

The girls' feet pound down the steps, then almost immediately pound up again. Their high-pitched voices are beaks, pecking and jabbing at his gray matter. He reels, grips the counter to steady himself.

Then he sits down stiffly and watches his daughters at the foot of the Christmas tree. Eyes beady, nostrils steaming, they grab their gifts, dig their nails beneath the ribbons and pull and rent. Dogs dismembering a fox, yes. Or vultures ripping open the stomach of an antelope. Each gift brings to their eyes a brief flame of satisfaction that dies out as they reach for the next. Hope, no hope. Hope, no hope. They keep looking and looking. It is not even Lin they are looking for anymore.

He decides to drive downstate with them and spend part of the Christmas vacation with Sidney and Violet, though he knows his parents' house will be more restful than his own. And he is right — Violet's shrill voice lights into her husband on the slightest pretext, chiding him beet-faced. Increasingly, Derek notices, Sidney seeks refuge in ditheriness.

He is dazed, watching them. What would he and Lin have been like after forty years of marriage?

You have never been married?

Lin jumps guiltily and the word No crosses her lips before she has time to think. She is having coffee with her seamstress, a sallow-skinned, magic-fingered Spanish woman, in the coffee shop of their Geneva hotel. They had been going over the fine details of her costume for tomorrow's performance — and then, out of the blue, this question Ah, then you could not understand . . .

The woman averts her eyes and Lin realizes she is about to hear the tale of a tragedy, yes that is what comes out, the woman is telling her how she had a little boy — Juanito, her youngest, the loveliest most adorable child, a real angel, look — she is actually pulling a photo from her bag stroking the dark soft curls with her index finger

and now with all her might Lin is not listening, she is managing to catch only shreds of the doleful litany . . . Last summer . . . riding his bicycle . . . quiet street . . . drunken driver . . . sixty miles an hour . . . rammed . . . skull split . . . The woman is staring at her now, forehead furrowed, eyes red, begging for recognition of her agony

but Lin maintains a steely silence

she is biting the insides of her cheeks so hard that the blood trickles down her throat.

Derek is on the bridge with Angela and Marina. The river is frozen over. All three of them are throwing stones onto the ice, laughing at the unexpectedly musical sound they make as they skate downstream.

A whole year has gone by. Derek looks at the girls and thinks: Lin has become a part of their past.

Lin is in Saint Moritz, Switzerland, where Nijinsky gave his final and terrifying public performance

his feet, world famous for their birdlike bones, scarcely touching the floor

just barely grazing it, dusting its face with magic

January 1919: Nijinsky was thirty and, the earth having recently opened up to receive the bodies of eight million young men, he now had no choice but to acknowledge weight. *One must have children in order that there be soldiers,* he wrote, *and now, as ashes cover the earth, we are exterminating them.* Dressed in white pajamas and black slippers, Nijinsky had danced all the horrors of the Great War — dodging bullets, stepping over putrefying corpses, getting his feet stuck in blood-soaked mud and finally — wounded, in agony — tearing his clothes to shreds in front of a thunderstruck audience. Then he had begun to painstakingly stack invisible wooden blocks on top of one another — what was he building? His imaginary castle toppled to the ground and he started over, block by block, carefully balancing, adjusting, praying that this time . . . or perhaps the next . . .

Lin has asked for bars. Not only horizontal ballet barres but vertical bars as well, and diagonal bars, slanting and intersecting in a fantastic jungle-gym across the stage. And as the orchestra plays Stravinsky's *Story of a Soldier* she dances Europe, the thing Nijinsky had tried so hard to build, or to rebuild — *I want there to be no more wars,* he had written, *no more borders.* The borders try to hem her in. She shimmies up a vertical bar and hangs from it at right angles,

does her exercises as if there were no such thing as gravity . . .
But as soon as her movements begin to flow into dance, the
bars are there to stop her and she must twist her body to fit
the shapes they draw. Her arms crook at awkward angles, her
knees buckle and warp, her head falls to one side, she is an
automaton, a broken soldier going through rote movements
that get faster and jerkier, jerkier and faster until she is banging violently into nothing at all — the bars now closing in
on her are invisible but they surround her more and more
tightly and relentlessly until at last she is forced to lie down,
straight and still — they have aligned themselves into the
four walls of her coffin . . .

When she comes back out on stage for her curtain call,
the orchestra conductor awaits her with an enormous bunch
of blood red roses; handing it to her, he kisses her on the lips

a real kiss

she feels his tongue

as the ovation continues, the orchestra conductor keeps
his arm around her waist, even between bows

and she realizes that he is a man

a young man

a handsome and gifted young male person who has left
the taste of his saliva in her mouth

how odd . . . how odd . . . Derek's saliva didn't taste like that

Derek decides to throw a dinner party. He and Rachel spend an entire Saturday shopping and cooking for it and by the time their friends arrive they are tipsy on nothing whatsoever.

All the guests stay until two in the morning, eating and drinking and making merry. When at last they get up and put on their coats, lingering in the hallway to exchange a last spatter of gossip and kisses and handshakes, Rachel does not make a move to leave with the others.

They are at the bedroom window, very tired. Derek holds Rachel's thin body to him and says in a low voice,
I love you, Rachel.

She slumps against him.

They sleep.

In the morning while it is still dark, before the girls wake up, they make love.

The taste of Rachel.

The scent of lilac and sweat at Rachel's neck.

The black arch of Rachel's eyebrows.

The long fingers of Rachel in his mouth.

The crooked painted toes of Rachel.

The ribs of Rachel.

Rachel at her computer, wearing glasses.

Rachel grinning at him through the fog of her morning tea.

Please move in with us, says Derek. If you want to.

I want to, says Rachel. She removes her shoes and stands on his two feet and bites the bones at the base of his neck.

He does not mind her clothes being where Lin's once were, her brush and comb and makeup being where Lin's once were, her slippers and housecoat being where Lin's once were.

Lin's body has disappeared at last from his body, so Rachel's hands on his skin are not where Lin's once were.

Marina scrutinizes Rachel, follows her every movement with murderous eyes. She longs to grab a hammer and bash her face in, such a pointy sharp-angled face compared to Lin's floating-featured one. Or rip out her hair, whose raven blackness invades her dreams with a fearful beating of wings . . . I hate you, she says to Rachel, just as she had once said I love you to the waitress.

Some days she rolls on the floor, kicking and groaning. Derek cannot bear to hear his five-year-old daughter groan.

Lin gives the Nijinsky solo every night for two weeks, and then the conductor takes her to the Italian seaside for a rest.
I'm so tired, she tells him as he rubs tanning oil into her back.
Where are you tired? he murmurs with an accent, rubbing. Which part of you is tired?
My everywhere is tired, says Lin. The marrow of my bones. My fingernails and toenails. My eyes. My eyes are tired. The roots of my hair are tired, tired. Did you know that the energy a dancer expends on stage is equivalent of one, if not two heart attacks?
Really, is that true? says the conductor, caressingly.
Yes. When Nijinsky was in his prime, he'd collapse panting onto the stage at the end of every performance, the second the curtain went down. People said he looked like a poor, crumpled rose, curled tightly on himself with his hands pressed to his chest. They even claimed you could hear his heart thumping above the cries and acclamations of the audience.
My goodness, that is incredible, murmurs the conductor.

It is early morning in their hotel room and the orchestra conductor is kneeling on the floor, his dark head burrowed between Lin's legs. In the love they made the night before, knees and elbows kept sprouting where she had expected only music. Now the conductor is trying desperately with lips and tongue to make her happy.
How very odd, Lin keeps saying to herself.
Your sex is not a flower, says the conductor after a while in his deep accented voice. People should not compare this thing to

a flower. Let me tell you what it is like, you do not know it well enough. It is a landscape, *voilà*. An extraordinarily complex landscape of ridges and valleys with wild grasses growing everywhere. The colors are pink, deep red, and violet verging on maroon. Your sex is the earth, a formidable volcano —

Lin breaks in.

It has already erupted twice, she says softly.

I beg your pardon?

The handsome young face looks up at her, ugly, its skin glistening, its lips red and slack.

I have two children, Lin says. She cannot stop herself from saying it. She needs to see him recoil.

And he recoils. Yes. The orchestra conductor recoils.

Lin's two children are in her handbag. She carries their wallet photos with her everywhere but she no longer looks at them. During the first year she looked at them so often that now, whenever she thinks of her daughters, it is these photos she sees in her mind's eye. No more moving memories of their life together.

The little girls in the photographs are frozen, timeless, always smiling, always seven and four years old. At night, however, they kick and struggle inside Lin's handbag, trying to get out. Lin hears their muffled screams, she knows she should go over and deliver her babies before they stifle from lack of air, but she cannot move.

Angela has taught Marina everything she knows about arithmetic. Marina is fascinated by numbers — she draws them in the air, juxtaposes and combines them. She counts everything — days, minutes, mouthfuls of food, tree branches. Her nightly ritual has been transformed: she no longer pays attention to headlights; instead, to ward off nightmares, she sits up straight in bed, stiffens her entire upper body and slams heavily down onto her pillow, sits up and slams down, fifty-two times in a row before slipping her thumb into her mouth and falling asleep. Fifty-two is filled with hope because it is both the number of weeks in the year and twice the number of letters in the alphabet — and also, secretly, four times thirteen, the bad-luck number which she loves and which protects her. Her own body is a thirteen: two feet two knees two hips two hands two elbows two shoulders and a head. She only thinks about the hard parts of her body, never the soft parts.

Derek and Rachel are sitting in the sun on the front steps of the philosophy building.

I always think it's so brave of the blossoms to come out a month before the leaves, says Rachel, whereas they're infinitely more fragile.

Yeah, says Derek. It's as if an army were to send out the women and children in the front lines to clear the way for the men.

They both fall silent and then, her eyes still on the trees but her shoulder pressing against Derek's, Rachel says softly, Does Lin write to you sometimes?

She's only written once, says Derek. Quite a while ago, to the girls. Do you think it's because she feels guilty?

Guilty . . . says Rachel slowly, lighting a cigarette to give herself time to think. Yes, I'd say, knowing Lin — but not remorseful. It was one of our mottoes when we were sixteen — no remorse, ever.

I've always known there wasn't an ounce of remorse in her, nods Derek. That she was remorseless because she was motherless.

But not an ounce of cruelty either.

No. You're right.

There is silence during which they feel the shy warmth of the sun on their faces and breathe in inane whiffs of student conversation from the air around them. Then Derek adds in a low voice.

Will you marry me?

Rachel, who has just inhaled the smoke from her cigarette, chokes on it.

Funny, she says, coughing, I was about to ask you the same question.

My answer's yes; what's yours?

Mine's yes, too.

Then let's marry each other.

That sounds like the simplest way of settling it.

Okay? Says Derek.

Okay. I'll marry you and you marry me.

Is that a promise, young lady?

Are you positive you're not married to anyone else, young man?

I've got a paper to prove it. It's covered with ink smudges and spelling mistakes, but there's an official stamp on it so it should work.

Okay.

Rachel gets to her feet.

In the meantime, I've got a class to teach.

So go ahead and teach it, Fatso. Who's stopping you?

Derek. Seriously.

Rachel stares at him.

Seriously.

He stares back.

You know I can't be a mother to your children.

Rachel. Get this through your head. I love you deeply and absolutely. I want to live with you day and night. I hope for you to be not a mother but a Rachel to my children. Now will you please go in there and teach those youngsters how to distinguish between form and appearances?

Okay, okay, you don't have to get all het up about it, I just thought I'd ask.

Marina and Angela attend their father's wedding at the town hall, along with a half dozen of his and Rachel's colleagues from the university. In the restaurant where they go afterward to celebrate, Marina orders milk and promptly takes a large bite out of her glass. Nothing serious, nothing serious — with an astonished look on her face she spits out the piece of glass whole.

Is this some Jewish wedding custom my mother never told

me about? says Sean Farrell, and the rest of them shriek with relieved laughter.

Sometimes, pressing his hand to Rachel's stomach when they make love, Derek can feel his own sex through the thin trembling paper of her skin. Sometimes when he rears up behind her and seizes her sharp hipbones, he is afraid of breaking her in two. As much as couple with his new wife, he wants to pamper her, dress her warmly, put flesh on her and see her gray hair grow out.

Marina counts her footsteps between home and school; she cannot speak to Angela as they walk because it would throw out her calculations. She prefers the sidewalk to the street because she can take exactly one and a half steps per square of sidewalk whereas crossing the street sometimes takes her eighteen steps and sometimes nineteen, so that the total can be anywhere between eight hundred sixty-four and eight hundred seventy; she tries to land on eight hundred sixty-seven every time and when she fails there is a punishment, she is not allowed to go to the bathroom at school all day long

one day she wets her pants in the afternoon and had to find a punishment appropriate to this new crime — she won't be allowed to drink any liquids for three days, she decides

she wishes she could stop eating too, but that would draw people's attention

and no one must know

Marina, come and see!

Angela drags her stiff sister into the storage room and they go through the trunk of Lin's old clothes together, dressing up like ladies of another era and giggling at their reflections in the glass.

Angela is the only person who can make Marina laugh, the only one who has the right to touch her.

Weeks go past, then more weeks, and Derek realizes he still has not informed his parents of his remarriage.

She's an old, old friend, he says weakly to Violet over the telephone. I've known her since I first came to the university, she teaches in the same department.

A professor! Sidney, did you hear that? Derek's married to a professor in philosophy! What's her name?

Her name is Rachel, Derek sighs.

Rachel! Did you hear that, Sidney? Derek's married to a nice Jewish girl, and a philosophy professor thrown into the bargain! Sidney, go take the upstairs phone, you're bothering me. Oh, this one will give you a son, I can feel it in my bones. And what a son!

Is she a nice girl? asks Sidney.

She's terrific. You'll love her, Dad, says Derek. A bit on the skinny side, maybe.

Bring her down here for Christmas vacation, why don't you? says Violet. I'll fatten her up. Is she a good cook?

Mother, I have to go now, it's the girls' bedtime.

Do the girls like her?
Bye, Mother. Bye, Dad.

How, Derek wonders, will I ever manage to be one person again? He wishes he could throw his universe at Rachel's feet, but part of his universe was made by another woman and cannot be thrown, it is hanging by a string from Europe. So he sleeps badly at night, worries, overworks, his stomach gnaws at itself, his doctor warns of a pre-ulcerous condition.

Then one evening he is in his study and the telephone rings. Rachel is out, sitting on a podium somewhere.
Derek?

The shock is like an atom bomb seen on TV with the sound off. He cannot answer.
Derek . . . I'll be coming to New York in July.

Lin's voice is loud and clumsy, as if it needed to force its way through the recalcitrant muscles of her throat and larynx.
Do you think I could see the girls?

The mushroom cloud dissipates. Derek's heartbeats are wounded survivors running and limping in all directions. If you want, he manages to say.
Derek, do you hate me that much?

Lin's voice has grown flutey.
No, he says. No, I don't.
Will you let me speak to Angela?
Lin, it's too . . . sudden.

There is a long silence.

You've remarried. Is that it? says Lin.

Another silence. She still knows him. She still translates his words correctly.

I've remarried, but that's not it. It's just that the phone's a pretty violent medium . . . I'm still reeling myself.

Who is your new wife?

Lin's voice is almost squeaky now.

Do I know her?

Derek does not answer.

Do I know her? repeats Lin.

I married Rachel, he says at last.

Rachel . . .

Derek says nothing.

I'm glad for both of you, says Lin.

Yet another silence.

Are the girls doing all right?

They're fine. Both of them are fine. What about you?

Just men, no husbands, she answers, translating correctly again.

Her voice has grown hoarse.

You were the only husband, Derek. I meant it and I still mean it.

I can't go on talking like this, Lin.

I'm sorry . . . Yes. Good-bye. Tell the girls I'll write to them.

The promised letter arrives several weeks after Lin's phone call. It is short, so short that Rachel and Derek can guess how much it must have cost her.

My little girls — though I know you're not so little anymore — I hope you haven't forgotten me because I sure haven't forgotten YOU! — Here are some photos and dance programs to show you what I've been doing all this time — Did your Daddy tell you I'm planning to be in New York next July? — My darling Angela — my sweet baby Marina — I can't wait to give each of you a great big hug and to cover you with kisses — Your Mommy — Lin.

Derek reads the letter out loud to the girls at the breakfast table. When he has finished, Angela grabs a metal pot and its metal lid and marches around the kitchen, clanging them together like cymbals. Marina pretends to be absorbed in reading the back of a cereal box.

Derek stares at them. He is numb.

It is a thrill for the girls to spend two weeks with their mother in a hotel room in New York City. Every evening while Lin dances they watch television, and when she returns long after midnight, the three of them cuddle up together in the king-size bed. Lin always takes a double whiskey and a sleeping pill just as she leaves the theater, so she will not lie awake once her children have fallen asleep, thinking about their bodies, thinking about how long their legs have gotten or how their moles seem to be in different places. She notices that Marina still sleeps with her thumb in her mouth

They wake up late, order a scrumptious breakfast to be brought up to their room, giggle as they brush their teeth together and have spitting contests in the sink.

Marina watches her naked mother as they get dressed, furtively, from beneath her fringe of bangs. She register every detail — the muscled calves, the long neck, the astonishing line of vertebrae jutting up from her back, as even and distinct as buttons on a coat

In the afternoon they go on outings to the zoo or the aquarium

Lin introduces them to her dancers, teaches them snippets of European languages

it is all so exotic and splurgy and gay

What Derek sees stepping down off the bus are two tanned strangers, disguised from head to foot in gaudy clothes and bantering in monosyllables of Spanish.

How's Mommy? he asks them as they drive north through cornfields and billboards. He does not like to call Lin Mommy, but he refuses to say How is your mother.

She's gorgeous, Angela answers. Her skin's all brown. She gave us lots and lots of presents!

The presents are colored woven skirts and scarves, black mantillas, silver lockets and ivory statuettes, collected through four years of wandering.

She was very sad, says Marina in a loud voice.

She was sad?

Yeah. When she took us to the bus station this morning, her eyes were full of tears.

The seasons inch and fly, inch and fly by. The girls change. They no longer throw their arms around their father's neck, ever. Derek wonders on *what day* they did this for the last time.

In December they all attend a ballet performance starring Angela and though Derek moves not a muscle, though his hand remains clamped to hers on the arm of the theater seat, Rachel can feel him pulling away from her, straining toward his past and toward the future he had thought he would have with the mother of this graceful glowing child up on stage. Like her mother before her, Angela now knows how to move each of her vertebrae independently. The human spine is one of the most beautiful things in the world, Lin used to tell her students — often in the summertime, reading in his study with the windows open, Derek would hear her sonorous voice ring forth from the third floor — it's like a great flower that rises and blossoms. Your muscles contain the memory of movement but your bones are the part of you that really lasts, long after death. Think of a cobra, coiled at the base of your spine then lifting itself up, up, until the hood is spread — yes! And remember that your pelvis is the earth, it must be tilled and irrigated — all the energy comes from there, is gathered and knotted there and can then go pulsating outward — love your stomachs! I love your stomach, Derek would tell Lin in the evening, kissing it then lowering his mouth to kiss the wetness between her thighs, drinking from her deeply, gustily, mad with the joy of her arching body, his hands clutching the firm cheeks of her behind . . .

He had forgotten how much he had been in love with her, and suddenly he is flooded with contempt for the unrelenting efficiency of his life with Rachel.

After the applause, the curtsies and flowers and lockjaw smiling at other parents during the ordeal of congratulations and apple juice, they drive home with the two girls in the backseat. Derek detests Rachel both for knowing exactly why he is upset and for forgiving him; he stubbornly holds his tongue and so does she. Angela, elated but exhausted, for once has nothing to say. And Marina is her usual taciturn self. The car reverberates with an ugly silence.

That winter, Marina starts calling Rachel Mommy.

When the two of them go walking in the forest together, she advances rapidly and stiffly, head down, eyes on the ground.

Tell me again how your uncles and aunts were taken away to Auschwitz, Mommy, she says when they stop at the bridge.

In Rome the following summer, she obstinately calls Lin Lin; remains sullen and withdrawn throughout the week they spend together. Lin sees she has relinquished her thumb at last, but that her fingers flutter nervously and her hands flit across her body like anxious butterflies, picking at imaginary pimples on her face, smoothing her torso in a jerky downward movement, over and over.

One sweltering night, with Angela sleeping peacefully and Marina fitfully next to her, the three of them covered only by a sheet, Lin tries to elicit memories of herself at nine, herself at twelve — combing, sifting backward through the decades in an effort to enter her daughters' dreams —

but it is unbearably stuffy in the room, the window is wide open and scraps of song and laughter from a group of carousers in the square below keep tearing apart her reverie

so that at last she gets up to take an extra sleeping pill

and mercifully her mind clouds over

yes once again she succeeds in fending off the tears

The next day, before accompanying them to the airport, she buys the girls more presents — she cannot help it, cannot stop herself, she wants to be in their hair, on their hands and feet, all over their skin, she is the book their eyes will zigzag across for hours, the sweater that will keep them warm next winter, the soft silk lingerie pressing against their most private parts, the parts she and Derek used to clean with competitive gusto and which she is no longer allowed to see or know about

But immediately they have gone — as of the taxi ride back from the airport — the work floods into Lin like water through a lock and fills her utterly, utterly,
      almost.

Angela menstruates for the first time.

Congratulations, says Rachel, planting a kiss on her forehead. That's the red carpet your body rolls out to welcome you into womanhood.

That evening after dinner Marina goes straight to her room and closes the door

her fingers are butterflies, flitting and fluttering, lightly grazing the whole surface of her body, tickling her, bothering her, she must catch them

Going over to her chest of drawers, she finds a pin and begins to stab her fingertips

one by one, calmly, carefully

Hold still, little butterflies, she murmurs, fascinated by the tiny globe of blood that swells up on the pink skin, then bursts and runs — Stay there, stay, my ruby — but always the globe bursts and runs and she must begin again

If only she could keep them all! String them into a necklace for her sister!

afterward, she takes care to flush the bloodied tissues down the toilet

Derek feels increasingly crushed by academic routine, and by the thought of his own aging. When he shaves in the morning he is depressed by the gray-brown shadows under his eyes. Lin used to love to watch him shave. Why doesn't Rachel ever watch him shave? Why doesn't Rachel make him feel his every gesture is irreplaceable? And why is he so edgy all the time?

To take his mind off his problems, he accepts invitations to conferences at prestigious faraway campuses and returns from them despondent, his pockets filled with stupid little hotel soaps and jam jars for the girls.

After one of these trips, he arrives back in town by bus at noon, unshaven and disgruntled. Entering the nearest coffee shop, he sits down at the bar and orders beer and a sandwich, hoping his bad humor will dissipate before he goes home to Rachel.

Then he sees Rachel. Through the shifting crowd of hungry students and harried waiters he sees her, seated at a table in the far end of the coffee shop, alone with a man. Sean Farrell.

He cannot help himself. He slides down from the stool and lurches forward, unable to take his eyes off his wife, her large serious eyes and her moving lips. He staggers across the room toward their table. When will she notice him? Can't she sense that the man to whom she is married is coming closer and closer? Would she sense it if he were aiming a gun at her?

He is mistaken: when they finally look up at him their surprise is glad rather than guilty.

And yet he is right.

That evening as soon as the girls have gone to bed — there is no reading to them anymore, no helping them into their pajamas or calming their fears about nightmares any-more, no running upstairs in response to their One Last Hug anymore, nothing but a perfunctory kiss on the cheek and then good night — he pours himself an aggressively large whiskey and wheels on Rachel.

So why do you wait until I'm out of town to see Sean Farrell?

I don't wait until you're out of town.

You mean you see him regularly.

No, I see him irregularly.

And I'm supposed to think that's just fine.

Derek, I've never told you what you were supposed to think.

Derek does not know what to say. If he asks her whether or not she is sleeping with Sean, they will have sunk to the level of soap opera. He wants to beat her up. Are you sleep-ing with him?

Darling —

Rachel moves to put her arms around him and he shoves her away.

Are you sleeping with him?

Oh, Derek. His mother just died. He's awash in pain. He needed to talk to me.

Rachel's voice is low, discouraged.

You're just friends, is that it?

No.

Again he is brought up short.

For God's sake, says Rachel. What's the matter with you? I love you.

You still love Sean Farrell. After all these years, you still love him. That's what you're telling me, isn't it?

Yes.

Derek feels her eyes on him but he cannot look up, it is as if she had just brained him with a shovel. This is sheer hell, he thinks. I'm too old to suffer like this.

And you still love Lin, Rachel goes on softly.

He cannot answer her.

Derek, we can't kill the thing we did before. I don't want to hear you say Lin was a terrible mistake.

Again she presses her body to his and this time he does not push her away, this time he clings to her like a frightened little boy.

Angela appears in the doorway to Derek's study, blond hair matted, nightgown awry.

Can I talk to you, Daddy?

Hey, it's eleven o'clock.

I know, but I can't sleep. I've been thinking.

    He swivels his chair toward her and she climbs onto his lap

    long shapely legs now, her feet dangle almost down to his

What are you thinking about? he asks.

I want to quit ballet, Daddy.

What?

Yeah.

But your teacher says you're gifted —

I want to do theater. I'm sure of it now, I want to be an actress when I grow up . . . Please say it's okay.

    Derek pushes her gently off his lap.

You don't have to decide about that right this minute, do you? People can change their minds between twelve and twenty, you know.

I won't change my mind. I'm *positive.* Oh, I'm so happy, Daddy!

    She kisses him on the mouth and vanishes. Derek's fingers move to his lips, wet from his daughter's kiss.

What are you reading, Mommy?

    Rachel glances up. Marina is standing in front of her, slightly pigeon-toed, her straight brown bangs almost totally covering her eyes.

Kant.

Who's that?

A German philosopher who used to go out for a walk every day at exactly the same time. When his neighbors saw him go past their window, they could set their clocks by him.

Marina smiles.

What does he talk about? Can you read me some?

She sits on the rug at Rachel's feet, poised to listen as a cougar poises to leap.

On the surface the girls seem to be growing apart from each other — Angela diving headfirst into femininity, shaving her legs and underarms, brushing her lashes with mascara, declaiming her lines in the kitchen, bathroom and bed, while Marina cultivates a purely mental excellence, sinking her teeth into knowledge, winning prize after prize and even skipping a grade at school . . .

The affection between them, however, is a fortress that protects them both.

Lin is in Chicago. She does not, will not tire of all this, the international tours, the airplanes, the under- or over-heated rehearsal rooms, the makeup, the phony clinky jewelry, the costumes, the curtains and the stages, hundreds of stages, some too big and some too small and some God help us raked, slanted deliberately for audience perspective whereas the dancers must pretend their surface is horizontal, not slip, not lose their balance.

Dressing rooms are the same all over the world, dust and

sweat, sweat and dust, smell of feet and underarms and crotches, leotards caked with toe crud and costumes yellowed with perspiration, bodies bent, broken into fragments, rubbing their ankles, massaging their necks, complaining of cramps and bruises — no she does not tire of this because onstage these same bodies are suddenly, always, painless and partless: their joints dilate, their flesh grows light and transparent and the sweat on their slick skin turns into molten gold, they are musical instruments, vibrant angels, streaming luminous clouds. This is the birth, yes, this is the preserved miracle of being alive: the only way not to lose it is to show and show its loss . . .

One night, removing her makeup after the performance, Lin hears a timid knock at her dressing-room door.

A plump and dowdy young woman is standing in the hallway, her eyes sparkling with tears.

It was heavenly, she breathes. Excuse us for invading your privacy like this —

Ah, the woman is not alone — a small girl was hiding behind her and is now being pushed toward Lin. Go on dear, go on —

The girl is clutching a single long-stemmed rose. Her mother must have told her to give it to the dancer, but she is paralyzed.

Is that for me? How sweet of you . . .

Lin bends to kiss the child on the forehead and relieve her of her fragrant burden.

I used to take ballet lessons myself, the mother blurts out, blushing, when I was in high school. But — oh, Mrs. Lhomond — you're everything I ever dreamed of being! Thank you for existing. That's all I wanted to say.

The girl is about Marina's age, Lin has been thinking.

And then: no. Of course not.

The child is three. By now Marina is thirteen.

She draws back, nodding, and — without a word — gently closes the door in their faces.

Marina has grown several inches this past year but there is as yet no bleeding from inside of her, she is too thin.
Don't worry, sweetheart, Rachel tells her. I was just the same. You'll have to start eating a bit more, that's all.
I'm not worried, Mommy, says Marina.

And suddenly adds,
Women stopped having their periods in the concentration camps too, didn't they?

Rachel stares at her, petrified.
Don't talk nonsense, she mutters, looking away. There is absolutely no comparison.

Seated cross-legged on the floor in Angela's room, Marina watches her older sister putting on her makeup.
Who're you going out with tonight?
Dave. He's the best actor in the whole theater club. Tall, dark, the whole bit . . .

Angela artfully draws a beauty spot on her right cheek-bone.
And what do you do together?
We go to the movies and we don't watch the film.
And?
And, yes. And so on, and so forth. Life can be terrific, Sis. All you have to do is close your eyes and you see the most amazing things.
Doesn't it smudge your makeup?
Who cares?

On the way back from school the next day, Angela
abruptly grasps Marina's arm.
Can you keep a secret? she says
Sure . . . So what's it like?

Shy and proud at the same time, Angela hesitates,
blushes, smiles.
It warm, she says. It's so warm. It's the warmest thing I've
ever known. You'll see.

They walk awhile in silence.
Did you bleed? says Marina at last.
Not a drop, says Angela. Ballet probably took my maiden-
head ages ago.
And . . . are you in love with David?
Who cares?

The two girls laugh.

As soon as they reach the house, Marina bolts upstairs
and locks herself into her room
    stands in front of the mirror
    and begins to slap her face, first slowly, then more and
more quickly
    thick and fast the blows rain down on her cheeks
    and it's warm, oh it's warm

That summer, the summer following Angela's graduation and Marina's sophomore year in high school, the girls meet Lin in Berlin. They are too big by now, of course, to share a bed with their mother, they are as tall as she is and Angela's breasts are bigger than hers, these visits are beginning to get awkward

and this one will be the last

Lin returns from the theater at one in the morning and finds Angela alone in their suite, half asleep.

Where's Marina?

What? — pushing thick blond locks out of her eyes, peering at her watch — She isn't back yet? That's funny . . . She went down to buy some cigarettes around eleven, I guess I fell asleep . . .

Marina, where are you? The first time she had crawled out of the kitchen all by herself. Or was that Angela?

Marina, where are you? The day she got lost in the department store —

She's fifteen years old, she explains at the local police station.

The officer is annoyingly obsequious, having recognized Lin from her photo in today's paper.

Don't worry, Mrs. Lhomond, she cannot be far away. It is not a dangerous neighborhood, probably she is in some nice bar close by, listening to jazz. Please, stay calm, we shall do everything in our power to find your daughter. Have you a photograph that might help us?

Lin stares at him. The old old photo is the only one, still

in her wallet, still smiling the same smile pressed flat against the smile of her sister.

No! she says. It is almost a shout.

Angela comes up and puts a comforting arm around her mother's shoulder

and for the first time in her life, Lin feels old. She feels like Bess.

They do find Marina, at five o'clock in the morning, just as dawn is starting to blanch the street of the city. Lin hears her voice in the next room, low and furious — just like her father, she thinks, she lowers her voice when she's angry

I was taking a walk, don't people have the right to go for a walk in the country?

This *is* your mother? says the police officer, showing her the newspaper photograph.

No, replies Marina. Her voice is dry, detached. I don't even know this woman. I've never seen her before . . . Now will you please let me go?

In the next room, Lin has collapsed onto a chair

Papers are checked.

You see? say Marina, jubilant. I told you she wasn't my mother. *I'm a Jew!* Lhomond isn't a Jewish name. Have you started arresting Jews again in this country?

Angela bursts into the room and strides over to Marina, gazes into her face. Marina tries to avert her eyes, but despite all her efforts they return, as if hypnotized, to meet those of her sister.

The big clock ticks and ticks. The policemen are non-plussed. No one moves.

At last Angela says in a warm calm voice

Hey Sis, I'm the actress, remember? Come on, it's been a long night. Let's go home.

She holds out both hands, palm upward, and after a moment Marina's hands come to rest on them like exhausted birds.

There is a scraping.

That is the only word for it, a scraping. It begins one September, in Madrid.

When Lin walks, her right hip seems to scrape — as when a shovel unexpectedly hits concrete. Oh, a tiny shovel. And it only happens when she has been working too hard and is exceptionally tired.

It is scarcely worth mentioning.

So she does not mention it.

Marina that same September stomps back and forth across her college campus, head down, carrying a heavy bag of books. She neither sees nor speaks to the other students, vaguer to her even than the trees. The flaming red maples, the running-shoed girls, the golden bursts of ash, the earnest pimpled boys, the stunning stippled Morse-code mixtures of crimson and green are like glued-on backdrop trees and people in a puppet show.

In her dormitory bedroom, she reads alone and sleeps alone and studies alone for her examinations, bending over her desk and smoking furiously. There is nothing on the walls. Her only reason for being in college is the Shoah, understanding the Shoah, the idea that gave birth to it and those that were impotent to prevent it — yes the object of her ceaseless reading and writing and thinking is horror.

Why? Angela asks her.

Well, I guess because compared to *that*, my own suffering is nothing. Just nothing, you know? For example, remember when we visited the Eiffel Tower with Lin, we were going up at an angle in that awful crowded elevator, getting jerked and jostled back and forth, this big fat lady stepped on my foot with her spike heel and I started to panic . . . and then suddenly I said to myself, at least we're not in a cattle car in 1943! It works every time.

Each Saturday morning Marina takes the train to Manhattan. When she arrives in the fearful huff of Grand

Central, always Angela is there on time to meet her, always Marina catches sight of her sister's blond frizz, then narrows and narrows her field of vision until it frames nothing but that, oh Angela you are so lovely, so reassuring walking toward me, and the two girls embrace. Angela's flesh is warm and firm and Marina is anchored by it, there is no floating or fear left in the station once she has touched the body of her sister.

Have you eaten?

Marina shakes her head.

You look as if you hadn't eaten since the last time I saw you.

Angela sneaks her into the kitchen of the restaurant where she works and the two girls gorge themselves, giggling, on fried oysters, tomato slices, whatever happens to be lying around.

In the evening Marina watches Angela perform her latest stand-up comedy routine — sometimes in a club, more often in the bed-sitting-living room of her Union Square apartment, where silent unappreciative roaches make up the rest of the audience.

Okay, look, this one's about women's feet, okay? No words.

And in the space of three minutes, as Marina watches mesmerized, Angela is transformed from a ballerina, aghast to see blood pouring from her pointes when she removes them, to an ancient Chinese courtesan trying not to put weight on her bound feet, to a fashion model wobbling on insanely high heels —

You're a genius! Marina tells her.

She wishes they were children again dressing up and playing make-believe.

Often on Sunday evening, just as Marina is about to head back out to the suburbs, a man arrives to take Angela out.

The men are black and white and brown, they are young and not-so-young; some are dressed in suits and ties and others in torn blue jeans; all of them smile and say Pleased to meet you when they shake her hand.

Are you careful? Marina finds the courage to whisper to her sister one night on the doorstep. Please, please be careful — I don't know what I'd do if anything happened to you.

Am I careful? Angela repeats, crossing her eyes and sticking out her tongue. You bet I'm careful. Condoms are the first step on the path to condominiums, baby.

And she gives her sister a noisy kiss on the cheek.

Marina makes no attempt to keep track of the names of Angela's men. They are too numerous — interchangeable, as far as she is concerned. In general the world around her is of little interest to her. When her train hurtles northward through the gutted hungry drug-wrecked ghetto on its way back to the college campus, always she is buried deep in Primo Levi or Simone Weil. She reads constantly, head down, head down; her daily and weekly trajectories are as invariable as those of a prison convict.

One Sunday, Angela being busy, she makes an exception to this rule and decides to spend the afternoon at the zoo. Instantly she realizes it is a mistake. The trees are naked, the sky filled with wind and dust, even the bushes look somehow vile. Stiff as a board, Marina strides across the litter-scattered lawns.

A man goes past her, muttering obscenities and rubbing at his crotch. She walks faster, her scalp tingling with fear. Will he follow her? Touch her? Plunge a knife into her stomach?

But when at last she glances backward, there is no one.

Arriving at the lion's case, she yearns to be one of its bars — standing straight and immovable amidst the other rods of iron. And then

she sees what is happening in the cage.

The lion and lioness are growling, stretching, rolling, yawning, rubbing up against each other, nibbling and pawing each other, exciting each other with unspeakable slowness and magnificence

their dance exudes a sensuality whose beauty and gravity are extreme

Marina stands there, revulsed but unable to take her eyes off the coupling wild beasts.

I am here because Lin and Derek once tumbled in this way

Lin is in Paris now with her company and the scraping in her hip has not gone away, it has evolved and deepened into what now can only be called pain. She is in pain all the time. The shovel continues to dig and grate at night, costing her sleep. She cannot afford it — the engagements are lined up all the way across Europe for the next four months. She needs her limbs of fluidity and oily smoothness, she cannot go on with this tiny terrible twinge there, always, there

The French doctor speaks to her in English. The word he pronounces is arthrosis, juvenile arthrosis, and instantly Lin's blood turns to ice. But the prognosis, he assures her, is excellent.

We know how to operate on these things, nowadays.

You'll be walking within a month.

Walking within a month? repeats Lin. Her mouth is dry.

The doctor smiles at her, nodding, and she stares back at him. Her eyes register the air of benevolence and superiority, the white teeth gleaming from beneath a gray mustache, the glasses perched on a hawk nose. She will remember this person. He has just pronounced the death sentence of her career.

What do you remember about Lin? asks Angela one Sunday morning in a midtown delicatessen, her pink lips brimming with bagels and cream cheese.

From before, you mean?

They have not seen their mother for more than two years.

Well, says Marina, I remember one summer we went out for a walk in the hills and she was wearing a pair of white shorts, she and I climbed up to the top of this steep hill together and then she held me between her legs and we slid all the way back down on our rear ends, and when we got to the bottom and stood up, Daddy pointed at the bright green stains on the seat of her white shorts and she laughed and laughed — do you remember that?

No, says Angela.

I wonder why I remember that, says Marina. What about you?

Oh, says Angela, it's not the same for me. I remember lots of things.

But what, for example?

Angela reflects.

Well, sometimes I'd go up to the dance room and watch her working with her dancers. She'd be sitting on the floor, staring at them and nodding her head in time to the music, and I'd see her in profile — beautiful, riveted — and realize I simply wasn't there for her. Nothing, not even the house on fire, could have made her turn away from those bodies — her eyes were *making* them dance, you see, bending them backward and forward, sweeping them left and right . . . Yeah. The intentness of her gaze, that's what I remember best. I couldn't believe she'd ever come back to earth again, recognize me and smile at me . . .

The waitress refills their coffee cups and Angela stirs sugar into hers, smiling dreamily.

Do you remember going to her father's funeral? she asks.

No, says Marina.

You got her new trench all covered with mud and she was furious.

She was furious with me because I got mud on her trench coat?

Angela looks at Marina's wounded incredulous face and burst out laughing; at last Marina gives in and laughs too and the two sisters repeat, over and over, laughing hysterically: She was furious with me because I got mud on her trench coat?

Lin stares down at her body stretched flat on the hospital bed, long long long in the pale green cotton gown

she wiggles her bare toes which seem miles away

I haven't been in a hospital since Marina

It is early morning, birds twitter noisily as a nurse
approaches to administer the anaesthetic, her brown eyes
warm and worried

I'm so sorry, Mrs. Lhomond, she whispers in French, bending over Lin.

When Lin re-emerges the birds have stopped twittering
and night has fallen. She feels nothing at all.

Her dancers come to visit her in the hospital. Flowers,
candies, kisses and reassurances — everything is far too sweet.
This is one of the snappiest bits of surgery in modern medicine, they tell her. A ninety-nine percent success rate. You'll
be on your feet in no time.

She has a new plastic neck for her thigh bone. She can
see it on the X rays. She studies the X rays thoughtfully, long
after the nurses have paid her their final visit for the night.

Every morning she goes to her rehabilitation sessions with
grim obedience; the crutches are rapidly replaced by a cane.

and then yes, she can walk again

she can walk

the medical personnel congratulate her, shake her hand,
wish her well

She catches up with her company in Copenhagen, they
are all there at the airport to meet her, all the well-known

well-loved faces. Coming out of customs, she sees them making a conscious effort not to watch the way she walks, not to notice how bad the limp still is.

Three cities later, in Munich, she must acknowledge that something is wrong. Despite her disciplined regime of rest and careful exercise the pain is not better but worse, every day worse. German X rays reveal the French surgeon's error: the neck of the thigh bone he inserted into Lin's body is a full three centimeters too long.

She can sue, of course, the German doctor assures her — and he can reoperate, of course — but the bone has suffered damage that by now is irreversible.

They are in their underwear sitting on Angela's bed in Manhattan, and Marina is weaving her sister's hair into dozens of skinny blond braids.

Suddenly Angela leaps from the bed, braids bobbing and exclaims,
I just had an idea for a new routine. It's about a mother who leaves her kids.

She closes her eyes for a moment to sharpen her concentration, then glues a serious, self-abnegating expression to her face and begins.
I did it for their sake, she says. Everyone's always complaining about invasive mothers, manipulative mothers, smothering mothers — well, I didn't want to be like that. I wanted *my* children to be strong, free, independent. So I let go of them — and look how wonderfully it all turned out! Johnny got his driver's license at age four, Susie got her Ph.D. at eight — now that's what I call *independent!* I'm so proud of them . . .

Marina's laugh rings out, too loud to be genuine. Stretching her hand toward the pack of cigarettes on the night table, she extracts one and lights it.
It's so weird, isn't it? she says after a moment, smoke mingling with the words as they leave her mouth. If you just imitate adults long enough, you end up turning into one.

Angela chortles in assent. She looks at her sister with tenderness.

Well, die and let live, that's my motto, sighs Marina with an exaggerated shrug.

Both of them laugh this time.

Once a month or so, they drive upstate together to visit Derek and Rachel. The trip takes two hours and invariably Marina is contented next to Angela at the wheel, Angela chattering and chewing gum and humming along with the radio while Marina smoke cigarettes, her feet on the dashboard.

They park in the driveway next to the big old house and honk the horn. Two people emerge to greet two people. First Rachel embraces Marina and Derek Angela, then the other way around.

Rachel is quite gray now and wears glasses when she reads, Derek has acquired a paunch and is starting to lose his hair; the girls are hurt to see their father and stepmother imitating the most conventional signs of middle age.

Rachel and Marina are walking in the woods, arm in arm, the day is dark November and they can see their breath. Then, standing on the bridge, Rachel says softly, her eyes resting on the black wriggling line of water,
You know darling . . . Sean Farrell is dying.
Oh, Mommy, breathes Marina. I'm so sorry.
He has lung cancer and he's dying and I still love him.
I know . . .
He's forty-nine years old and he knows he's dying and there's nothing anyone can do. And I hate it when our friends say he shouldn't have smoked so much.
Yes.

Marina squeezed Rachel's shoulder through her heavy winter coat.

Do you think Lin slammed the door when she left?

Marina asks Angela as they drive back to the city together in the pouring rain.

No, I don't think so.

You think she closed it after her very softly.

Yes.

The wipers drive great shivering curves of rain into the corners of the windshield.

Knowing it was the last time.

Yes.

And . . . do you think she kissed us good-bye that morning?

Yes.

There is a pause, the car is warm, the windshield wipers beat like a heart.

Was it hard for you?

Angela frowns.

It's funny, she says. I think what hurt the most was her things. I always loved her things, you know? Touching her dresses and her underwear, borrowing her jewelry, fiddling around with her bottles of perfume and nail polish . . . All of those *things* just disappeared, you know? Just gone! That's what I remember. The empty shelf in the bathroom. The empty dresser drawers . . . Her smell hung in the air for months and months.

Lin does not cancel her company's engagements; rather she reworks the choreographies, cutting her own body out of them.

Marina copies into her notebooks the most troubling passages from her readings. She has learned a great deal. She has learned that some mothers in the camps, when they were certain the gas chamber was for tomorrow, slashed their daughters' wrists during the night.

Marina tosses and turns in her dormitory bed. What did the mothers *use* to accomplish this act of mercy? There couldn't possibly have been glass glasses in the barracks, no bottles either — where on earth did they find the cutting instruments with which to prove their love?

The only nights Marina sleeps well and deeply are those she spends in her sister's foldout bed in Union Square, with its fluffy pillows and eiderdown quilt. Angela sleeps in the nude and Marina, wearing black silk Chinese pajamas, presses up against her sister's body and falls asleep with her head on her sister's breast.

It is January and the city too is draped in eiderdown, the city too is tossing and turning beneath its quilt of white . . . I have a surprise for you, announces Angela at breakfast.

The surprise rings the doorbell an hour later. It is two men, one for each of them.

Angela has chosen judiciously — the man she has selected for her sister is someone big and warm, like a big warm comforting bear. The other man, the one Angela herself is currently in love with, has a wife and several children. That day the four of them have a sparkling snowball fight in Central Park and

then hot chocolate afterward and from then on, every weekend, the comforting bear is there for Marina.

The four of them double-date. They go out to movies
and to restaurants, drink and talk and laugh so much that
Marina begins to wonder if she too is falling in love. She
watches Angela radiate in the presence of her lover, then
glances at her own big warm bear of a man and blushes and
averts her eyes not yet daring to radiate herself. When his
large brown hand touches her face, it is like a hammer being
used to brush away a feather and she flinches

but he is slow and careful with her, knows he is the first
and must not frighten her

When they are alone together they talk far less than
when they are with Angela and her lover, but he tells her he
admires her silence, knows that it contains worlds of wisdom

and her marks at college seem to bear him out. She com-
pletes her freshman year with flying colors

and then, one chilly October Saturday in her sophomore
year, he drives up to her college and takes her north along the
coast, with country-and-western on the tape deck filling the
car. They park by the Atlantic Ocean and the warm bear
explores the cavern of her mouth with his tongue as the
motor and heater and music continue to thrum, but when he
presses her hand to his arousal she is choked with nausea and
cannot, no simply cannot

rigid with tension, she insists he drive her back to the campus

will not let him touch her again, see her again

After this she sticks to her studies. No more fooling around, she tells herself. There is so very much to be understood. Not only her days but her nights are spent indelibly engraving on her brain the images of deportation and death camps, crushed ghetto uprisings, hunger, blood, smashed skulls of babies. She feels she is a light that must go into that darkness, explore its farthest reaches, plumb its depths

and in order to be this pure light she must avoid taking on material substance. Her rules about eating and sleeping grow increasingly stringent. The constant pain at the back of her head, the dull ache of hunger in her stomach are stimulants to her as she works through the night. The less she eats, the better she can concentrate.

Irregularly, Rachel and Derek write to Lin, short sporadic letters which, when they finally catch up with her after leapfrogging from address to forwarding address, keep her more or less abreast of the family's news.

In this manner Lin hears of Sidney's death

Violet's purchase, thanks to the savings of her dear departed, of a house in Florida

Angela's first tour on the club circuit

Marina's extraordinary term paper on the notion of evil in Heidegger and Arendt

Rachel's early menopause

Derek's freshly cauterized ulcer

She herself sends mostly postcards, none of which make any mention of her hip.

Lin is in Tokyo, the country of *Madama Butterfly*.

The great Pavlova had danced with butterflies as a child. Years later, when she performed her forty-second butterfly solo — standing on tiptoes and beating her fingers and eyelashes with inhuman lightness and velocity — the entire hall would be electrified, vibrating, filled with tiny, whirring wings . . . But Lin is working on *Butterflies of the Night:* she has taken Nijinsky's last, unrealized choreography and brought it to fruition.

Her hair has been dyed gray and yellow. Seated in front of her mirror backstage, wearing a shapeless flowered dressing gown, she smears rouge heavily onto her cheeks, daubs her eyelids with purple, draws deep wrinkles onto her forehead, stretches her lips into an enormous artificial smile. Then she stares at herself. No, it is her character who stares at her and acknowledges her — all right, you have the right to embody me.

When the curtain goes up, the prostitutes are wrapped tightly in their cocoons, prostrate on the floor. The sun crosses the sky to discordant music and as the shadows slowly thicken, the whores begin to wriggle and squirm like worms. Emerging from their hot sticky blankets they shake themselves, ready themselves for the night's flight. They put on flounced and frilly dresses, jangling jewelry, garish makeup — but they have no faces, they are masked and it is the masks which they meticulously make up.

Lin is the madame, the once-beautiful cocotte, now aged and paralyzed. She has seen everything, she is a specialist of the ephemeral — poor passions, false hopes, ardent illusions — but she continues to do her job. At center stage, hideous and indomitably powerful in her wheelchair, she choreographs the traffic of love, selling girls to boys, youth to age, woman to woman, man to man.

The restless bodies pull and push, ram and slam, execute motions of unutterable lyrical tenderness then switch without warning to brutal obscenity, reach heights of physical harmony worthy of Michelangelo then plummet into public toilet clawing. The masked butterflies flit fitfully around the stage, coupling and separating and coupling again, beneath the weary all-knowing gaze of their mistress.

Angela no longer needs to wait on tables or sleep with seven different men in order to pay her rent. Her stints as a comedienne, if not regular, are lucrative now, and she continues to be happy with her married lover

so happy that when a baby begins to grow inside of her she lets it grow.

But what will you do with it? asks Marina as her sister's stomach swells and swells. Where will you put it? How on earth are you going to look after it?

Angela's wide grin only widens further, as if the child she was carrying carried in itself the answers to all the possible questions in the world.

Over the next six months, Rachel follows the agony of Sean Farrell in the state of helpless rage. She needs to talk to someone about it and there is only one person in the world who can understand.

I went over to his place last week, says the letter which reaches Lin in Tokyo. *We had lunch together and he joked about his angel wings having been torn off . . . I can't fly anymore, he said. I'll never fly again . . . He's already had two operations. They have removed the left lung completely and then a new nodule formed on the right so they removed a piece of that too and now he can't breathe anymore . . . He took off his shirt and showed me the symmetrically curved scars on his back, beneath the shoulder blades. And he was right — it looked as if he'd had wings and somebody had torn them off and then sewn up the place where they'd been attached. Then he turned around and showed me his naked chest . . . His breasts are swelling and he has shooting pain in his nipples all the time. He smiled at me. Look, he said, they're turning me into a woman. And then he asked me to touch his breasts. So I cupped my hands around them . . . very gently, very carefully . . . and then I said, Now you touch mine . . . Do you understand, Lin? He took my breasts in his two hands, and he just stood there with his eyes wide open and the tears pouring down his face —*

That evening there is no performance; Lin goes out and wanders at random through the streets of Tokyo, leaning on her cane. Everything she sets her eyes on — every bicycle, storefront, neon sign, restaurant, office building, human face, pebble, gutter, taxi — is a thing which Sean will never see. This city and all cities are about to be withdrawn from him. *The world.* From now on, all the deserts, jungles, sunsets, seasides, mountains, heaths of the world will be places Sean is not. No more reality for Sean, and no more Sean for reality . . .

She wanders the better part of the night, losing her way repeatedly, awakening the old pain in her hip. She thanks the pain for reminding her she is in the world, a world made sublime by its sheer existence.

Marina is with Angela in New York when her labor begins, there are no men in sight.

Do you realize, says Angela, that I remember when Lin left for the hospital to have you?

No, says Marina, that's impossible. You were only three, how could you remember?

Angela grimaces in pain before replying. She is busy packing the last items from the list into her suitcase.

I remember she took a bath and I said Are you having the *concracktions,* Mommy? and she said I sure am!

No, says Marina firmly. You must remember her telling you you said that later on.

They inch through the Greenwich Village traffic in a taxi, Marina holding her older sister's hand. Every few minutes, Angela's entire body tenses and she crushes Marina's fingers.

What does it feel like? whispers Marina when the pressure on her hand subsides.

I'm glad you're here, Sis, says Angela.

Marina's head begins to spin.

I'll stay with you in the delivery room, if you like, she says.

I'm glad you're here, repeats Angela, because I just had an idea for a new routine. Listen. It's this ambulance driver, see, an ambulance driver who likes to take things easy. I mean, he's really a laid-back dude. He's got this mashed-up accident case in the back, his siren's wailing, and he's driving down Fifth Avenue at about, uh, ten miles an hour, he sees this green light and he says to himself Wow, that light looks to me like it's about to turn *yellow,* man, so he slows down to two miles an hour and sure enough, after a while the light does turn yellow so he says to himself, Well, I might as well just stop. And while he's stopped at the red light this taxi pulls up beside him, it's a nice day, you know, they've got their windows rolled down — Hi! How're you doin'? You hear the way that game turned out last night? Yeah, man . . . unbelievable. The mangled person in the back is groaning and bleeding all over the place but the ambulance driver starts feeling a bit thirsty, so when he gets to Washington Square he decides to stop off for a drink at the Cedar Tavern. He double parks at the curb, his siren still wailing and all, and saunters into the bar — Hi, guys. How's tricks? Yeah, I'll have a Bud. Scratches his stomach. Lights up a cigarette . . . Oh, thanks. Takes a long swallow, smacks his lips . . . Mmm, that's *good* . . . Well, gotta be goin', I got somebody waitin' for me in the —

A contraction forces Angela to break off, knuckles pressed to her teeth. When the pain subsides, she says
Is that funny, Marina? Do you think that's funny?
Sure it is, Angie, That's real funny. It's great.

Angela screams.
You're doing fine, says the doctor, I can see the head already — there it is!
Really? says Angela, laughing and crying and steaming with sweat. Really? You can see it?
You bet I can, and wow, has this kid ever got a thick head of hair! Look, she adds, beckoning to Marina.

Marina's brain is doing cartwheels in her head. She closes
her eyes and whispers,
Lots of hair . . .
Angela screams.
Push, says the doctor. Go ahead, push with all your might, all
systems go.
Now it is Marina's hand that crushes Angela's. Even with
her eyes closed she can see the dripping blood, the inhumanly
straining face, the orgasmic embrace of savage pain and savage joy . . .
So first you push us out between your legs and then you
push us away — I need to dance — the dancer who redis-
covered the floor — So eat the floor, Mom, you like the fucking floor so much, go ahead, eat it, chew the linoleum —
You're all dried out, Mother, nothing but skin and skeleton,
dry gooseflesh now and empty rooster skin, a dessicated soul
filled up with sand and silt and smoke — Oh, your wooden
flautists, huffing and puffing into hollow desert flutes, dry
drum and dry guitar, pluck pluck pluck the strings, pluck the
feathers one by one — Mexico cacti spines in your cunt —
eagle beaks pecking at your eyes — great white skulls with
gaping eyeholes, clattering teeth — desert sun singeing life to
ash — burn it all yes let the blood run dry, let the skin be
emptied — Dry our Mom, burn out — dry red cliffs like
rows of grinning teeth, teeth, death mother death mother
death death death —
and then the child shoots forth in a triumphant spew of
red blue violet, there is the thick twisted cord of flesh being

snipped and the heavy handful of placenta being extracted and Marina too is screaming but it is dream screaming, screaming without sound, she must not vomit or fall to the floor with flailing arms and legs, oh God this thing is a person, these viscous shapes are human limbs, these slimy lumps at the crotch are genital organs, this thing is a boy.

The child is named Gabriel, after no one in particular.

It is Marina who telephones Derek and Rachel to inform them they have become grandparents.

A few days later, she returns to her college and resumes her maniacal processing of words. There will be less room for her from now on in Angela's apartment, less time for her in Angela's busy schedule.

Angela find a young Puerto Rican woman to look after her baby evenings while she works. His father can scarcely feed his legitimate offspring as it is, so he will not be able to contribute much to this bastard's upkeep; he continues, however, to be deeply in love with Angela and this is all that matters.

One morning in the middle of an exposé on Nietzsche, Marina collapses in a faint in front of the entire class. Upon regaining consciousness in the infirmary, she denies being ill so adamantly — I'm perfectly fine, really — it's nothing at all — there's no point in alarming my parents — that she is released without further questioning.

Then her mother is in the Sunday supplement.

Not Rachel, Lin.

The letters are there, Lin Lhomond black on white, along with a color photograph, a recent shot of her mother's body, the body she, Marina, once lived in. Will soon be arriving in New York. With her international dance company

her smile

how dare she smile at the camera?

Rising abruptly in her dormitory room, Marina strides to the mirror and holds the photo of her mother next to her own face.

Lin Lhomond has lost her beauty, that much is clear.

Hey Angie, says Marina thickly over the telephone, you feel like going to watch Mom dance?

Didn't you read the article? says Angela. She doesn't dance anymore.

Marina shakes her head no, as if her sister could see her. She had a hip operation in Paris, Angela continues, and the doctors screwed it up. She's walked with a limp ever since.

Marina goes on shaking her head, shaking her head.

She only does choreography now, adds Angela.

Marina's hands tremble as she dials the number of the theater where Lin's company is performing.

But I'm her daughter! she insists when the arch Manhattan voice dismisses her request. She didn't know I was going to be in town! All I want is the name of her hotel!

The lump in her throat makes her sound like a liar, a frustrated fan.

Sorry, Miss, the voice says coolly. We're not allowed to give out any information concerning the artists.

Days dribble by and for the first time in her life Marina is unable to concentrate on her studies. She knows there is something, something — but how

And then Rachel telephones and says, her voice streaked with tears

Marina it's Mommy —

What . . .

Marina, darling, Sean Farrell just died.

And Marina suddenly sees how.

She stand in line five hours and purchases the last cancellation ticket to the final performance.

Packed tight in the overheated theater the audience is spellbound, and Marina's icy hands clutch the program overflowing with her mother's name. Heart pounding, head splitting, she watches the dancers do what her mother has told them to do.

The dance is about aging. Lin has known since she first set out that the career of a dancer is a miniature, mercilessly compressed version of a human life, and here she has compressed it even further, fitted it into the space of a single evening, this same arc from youth to death, seen not from the outside as loss of beauty but from the inside, the secret lubricated inner workings of the flesh, her dancers are cells of nerve and muscle, they are bones and corpuscles first expanding, electric with vitality, then slowing growing turgid, tripping and bumping into one another, yes sickening — but beautifully, beautifully — dancing the inevitability of infection and decline, sculpting arteriosclerosis and varicose veins, the jerks and spasms of neurone damage — but beautifully — yes, this, too — accept, accept this music too, this betrayal, the powerful dissonance of this defeat.

At last what Marina hoped for happens — amidst the roars of bravo and the earthquakes of applause, Lin Lhomond in the flesh and blood, holding the hand of the orchestra conductor and surrounded by her dancers, limps out into the middle of the stage takes a bow. So here she is. So here I am in the same room with her. The audience rises to its fee and Marina rises too, then moves slips flows into the aisle as the curtain gradually comes down.

Lin is alone in her dressing room as always after a performance; the knock on her door makes her jump and swear under the breath. Who on earth —
What is it?
She peers hostilely into the half light
then, recognizing her daughter, exclaims, draws her into the room, clasps her stiff body briefly to her own
but Marina pulls away

always

always she refused to be comforted, cuddled, even as a baby

You came to see the show? says Lin.

Marina nods, lights a cigarette and sucks on it as if it were a thumb, her arms folded tightly across her chest.

Did you like it?

Silence. Lin glances involuntarily at her dressing table — there is a small bottle of brandy standing where her jars of makeup used to stand — but she refrains from pouring herself a drink, turns her back on her daughter and moves to the window.

When Marina speaks her voice is high and wintry.

I can't understand, she says. I'll never understand.

Lin shrugs and stares into the black New York night. Time goes by.

Should Isadora have worn a shorter scarf? she murmurs at last. If she had, she wouldn't have been Isadora.

At least she strangled herself, replies Marina instantly. Whereas you strangled us. Better to have done it at birth and gotten it over with.

Anger courses through Lin's bloodstream — a relief.

Is that why you've come here? she says, struggling to keep her voice firm. To display your pain to me? You're so proud of it, aren't you, Marina? No one can take it away from you, no one can come near it — you'll never relinquish it, will you? You must always be bleeding out there in the open.

Another silence.

No. Marina says finally. As a matter of fact I didn't come here to display my pain. I came to tell you an old friend of yours just died.

Lin freezes. She knows the words that will come next.
Sean Farrell. Do you remember him?
Of course.
I'm sure it would mean a lot to Mommy . . . I mean . . . Rachel . . . if you came to the funeral. It's on Sunday afternoon, the day after tomorrow — we could all drive up together, the three of us. Angie's got a car. She's also got a baby, in case you're interested. His name is Gabriel.
All right, says Lin at length. I'll come.

They are in the car, yes, all four of them are riding along in Angela's car, tiny Gabriel gurgling next to Marina in the back and Lin up front next to Angela who is at the wheel. Marina leans forward so that her head is between her mother and her sister and she can follow their conversation, which is about stage fright, their respective ways of dealing with stage fright

the roads are icy and treacherous and the trip takes longer than usual. By the time they arrive, the funeral procession has left Sean Farrell's house and is advancing toward the Catholic church

Derek, taking the soft bundle of Gabriel in his arms, looks at Lin and his eyes suddenly fill with tears

Rachel, aged and overwrought, throws her arms around her childhood friend and hugs her with such desperation that Lin is almost knocked off her feet

together they enter the church

after the oratory Lin limps to the coffin, makes the sign of the cross over it with the incense burner, limps back to her seat

it would be silly for her to stay anywhere else but in the old house

these details don't matter anymore, far too many things have happened, there's no point in standing on ceremony, is there, given their acute awareness that they will more or less shortly be joining their old friend Sean in the dust . . .

Come home with us, says Rachel simply

and so they all set out on foot, Derek and Rachel and Lin walking a few yards in front of Marina and Angela who wheel Gabriel's baby carriage through the miserable February dusk. Rachel is swaying with loss and Lin is limping, so Derek takes the arms of both his wives and they advance thus, arm in arm in arm

and when they reach the dear old house, when they have shut out the icy air and wended their way in single file into the living room, Lin draws three bottles of vodka from her overnight bag

Straight from Moscow, she says, relishing the way Rachel's eyes widen in astonishment, then crinkle into mirth.

Theresa has stacked kindling and logs in the fireplace and laid out a light supper

That evening the five of them get drunk together, as Gabriel sleeps and sleeps

It's a family reunion! says Derek at around eleven, when they finish the first bottle.

Everyone laughs uproariously, including Marina

much later still, when almost nothing is making sense anymore, when Billie Holliday is singing in the tired cracked heartbreaking voice of her final months, and Angela is floating dreamily around the room with her eyes closed and her arms waving, and Marina is smoking a cigarette all the more blissfully that it has just this afternoon been proved to her that cigarettes indeed can kill, Lin leans over to Derek and kisses him full on the mouth

It was so strange, she says, looking at Rachel tenderly but not apologetically, so very, very strange to kiss a man again . . .

after having been through all that . . . Do you know what I mean, can you imagine?

Rachel squeezes her old friend's hand

Did you tell them you had kids? Derek asks her awhile later but Lin does not reply, she is staring into the fireplace, reminiscing perhaps about all the fires she built there, hundreds of fires in the course of eleven years . . . She feels very calm

everything is exceedingly calm

I can make you up a bed in your old dance room, if you like, says Rachel at last

That would be marvelous, says Lin. I think I must be tired. Yes, I am. I'm dead tired. Do the girls still sleep in their old rooms? she wonders inconsequentially

Oh, yes.

Well, well, well. It's an odd life, isn't it?

Derek nods, standing.

It's an odd life, he says.

Marina is calm now also. In her room, still decorated with her high-school diploma and certificates of excellence, she falls into a deep and dreamless, unprecedently wonderful sleep

then half wakes in the hush of dawn and crawls upstairs, up the second flight of stairs to where the star is sleeping, too, the star whose face is partially concealed by a dark and eyeless mask and whose left arm is flung out onto the floor next to the mattress

Marina crawls, she can see herself crawling in the wall of mirrors, crawling in her long white nightgown to the edge of the star's bed, then snuggling in between the sheets and cuddling up to the sleeping body, the sleeping liquor-leadened body with its plastic hip, the world-famous dead-tired body that has moved its masked and graying dreamless head away from the pillow and flung one arm onto the floor, the very floor on which it used so many years ago to dance, in front of these same mirrors — and Marina snuggles closer, pressing her body the length of her mother's body, then gently shifting the pillow and pushing it up against her mother's nose, her mother's mouth, repeating over and over in an ardent whisper, I love you, I love you —

the murder would be utterly painless

Lin tears her face away from the pillow that was stifling her
lurches out of bed in her Manhattan hotel room, feverish
and heavy headed,

limps to the bathroom, splashes her face with cold water
and raises it to the glass. Her eyes gaze into her eyes, they are
firm and clear and gradually she recovers from the dream —
she is used to this by now, more than used to it, inured to it.

As she is finishing her toilette the telephone rings — it
is room service, informing her it is eleven o'clock and her
breakfast is ready — the girls will be arriving at noon and
Sean's funeral is at three, dear sweet miserable Sean, the man
who once told me the university was nothing but a shattered
universe, of course the reverse is equally true, the universe is
nothing but a shattered university . . . I'll probably spend the
evening with Derek and Rachel . . . It will be strange, she
thinks, pausing as a piece of her dream twinges briefly in her
brain, extremely strange but marvelous to see them again,
they'll ask me to stay overnight in the big old house, perhaps
only out of courtesy, I'll reserve a bed-and-breakfast just in
case, but if they insist I'll stay with them, then catch the nine
o'clock bus out to Boston

she has promised her dancers to be on time for the afternoon run-through there.

Lin moves to the window. Three storys below, the human
world goes blindly about its Sunday business. Amorous cou-
ples stroll down the sidewalk, leaning into one another,

warming to luscious memories of the night before. A black nanny pushes a perambulator with a white baby in it. A church bell clangs loudly, summoning late sleepers to worship. A bus hurtles past in a spray of slush.

All this is mine

Ardenais, January 1992 — Cambridge, March 1994